THE END
OF NANA SAHIB
THE STEAM HOUSE

THE END OF NANA SAHIB

THE STEAM HOUSE

BY
JULES VERNE

AUTHOR OF "TWENTY THOUSAND LEAGUES UNDER THE SEA,"
"THE MYSTERIOUS ISLAND," ETC., ETC.

Translated from the French by
A. D. KINGSTON

Rupa & Co

This edition © Rupa & Co. 2011

Published 2011 by
Rupa Publications India Pvt. Ltd.
7/16, Ansari Road, Daryaganj
New Delhi 110 002

Sales Centres:
Allahabad Bengaluru Chandigarh Chennai
Hyderabad Jaipur Kathmandu
Kolkata Mumbai

All rights reserved.
No part of this publication may be reproduced, stored in
a retrieval system, or transmitted, in any form or by any
means, electronic, mechanical, photocopying, recording or
otherwise, without the prior permission of the publisher

Printed in India by
B.B. Press
C-243, Sector-4
DSIDC, Bawana
Delhi 110 039

CONTENTS.

CHAPTER I.
"Two Thousand Pounds for a Head" . . . . PAGE 1

CHAPTER II.
Colonel Munro 17

CHAPTER III.
The Sepoy Revolt 34

CHAPTER IV.
Deep in the Caves of Ellora 52

CHAPTER V.
The Iron Giant 67

CHAPTER VI.
First Stages 81

CHAPTER VII.
The Pilgrims of the Phalgou River 100

CHAPTER VIII.

A FEW HOURS AT BENARES 121

CHAPTER IX.

ALLAHABAD 141

CHAPTER X.

VIA DOLOROSA 156

CHAPTER XI.

THE MONSOON 157

CHAPTER XII.

THREE-FOLD LIGHT 184

CHAPTER XIII.

CAPTAIN HOOD'S PROWESS 200

CHAPTER XIV.

ONE AGAINST THREE 218

CHAPTER XV.

THE PÂL OF TANDÎT 238

CHAPTER XVI.

ROVING FLAME 250

CHAPTER I.

"TWO THOUSAND POUNDS FOR A HEAD."

"A REWARD of two thousand pounds will be paid to any one who will deliver up, dead or alive, one of the prime movers of the Sepoy revolt, at present known to be in the Bombay presidency, the Nabob Dandou Pant, commonly called . . . ."

Such was the notice read by the inhabitants of Aurungabad, on the evening of the 6th of March, 1867.

A copy of the placard had been recently affixed to the wall of a lonely and ruined bungalow on the banks of the Doudhma, and already the corner of the paper bearing the second name—a name execrated by some, secretly admired by others—was gone.

The name had been there, printed in large letters, but it was torn off by the hand of a solitary fakir who passed by that desolate spot. The name of the Governor of the Bombay presidency, countersigning that of the Viceroy of India, had also disappeared.

What could have been the fakir's motive in doing this?

By defacing the notice, did he hope that the rebel of 1857 would escape public prosecution, and the consequences of the steps taken to secure his arrest? Could he imagine that a notoriety so terrible as his would vanish with the fragments of this scrap of paper?

To suppose such a thing would have been madness. The notices were affixed in profusion to the walls of the houses, palaces, mosques, and hotels of Aurungabad. Besides which, a crier had gone through all the streets, reading in a loud voice the proclamation of the Viceroy. So that the inhabitants of the lowest quarters knew by this time that a sum, amounting to a fortune, was promised to whomsoever would deliver up this Dandou Pant. The name, annihilated in one solitary instance, would, before twelve hours were over, be proclaimed throughout the province.

If, indeed, the report was correct that the Nabob had taken refuge in this part of Hindoostan, there could be no doubt that he would shortly fall into the hands of those strongly interested in his capture.

Under what impulse, then, had the fakir defaced a placard of which thousands of copies had been circulated?

The impulse was doubtless one of anger, mingled perhaps with contempt; for he turned from the place with a scornful gesture, and entering the city was soon lost to view amid the swarming populace of its more crowded and disreputable quarter.

That portion of the Indian peninsula which lies between the Western Ghauts, and the Ghauts of the Bay of Bengal, is called the Deccan. It is the name commonly given to the southern part of India below the Ganges. The Deccan, of which the name in Sanscrit signifies "south," contains a certain number of provinces in the presidencies of Bombay and Madras. Chief among these is the province of Aurungabad, the capital of which was, in former days, that of the entire Deccan.

In the seventeenth century the celebrated Mogul Emperor Aurungzebe, established his court in the town of Aurungabad, known in the early history of India by the name of Kirkhi. It then contained one hundred thousand inhabitants. Now, in the hands of the English who rule it in the name of the Nizam of Hyderabad, there are not more than fifty thousand. Yet it is one of the most healthful cities of the peninsula, having hitherto escaped the scourge of Asiatic cholera, as well as the visitations of the fever epidemics so much to be dreaded in India.

Aurungabad possesses magnificent remains of its ancient splendour. Many artistic and richly ornamental buildings bear witness to the power and grandeur of the most illustrious of the conquerors of India, the renowned Aurungzebe, who raised this empire, increased by the addition of Cabul and Assam, to a marvellous height of prosperity.

The palace of the Great Mogul stands on the right bank of the Doudhma. The mausoleum of the favourite Sultana of the Shah Jahan, the father of Aurungzebe, is also a remarkable edifice; so likewise is the elegant mosque built in imitation of the Tadje at Agra, which rears its four minarets round a graceful swelling cupola.

Among the mixed and varied population of Aurungabad, such a man as the fakir above mentioned easily concealed himself from observation. Whether his character was real or assumed, he was in no respect to be distinguished from others of his class. Men like him abound in India, and form, with the "sayeds," a body of religious mendicants, who, travelling through the country on foot or on horseback, ask alms, which, if not bestowed willingly, they demand as a right. They also play the part of voluntary martyrs, and are held in great reverence by the lower orders of the Hindoo people.

This particular fakir was a man of good height, being more than five foot nine inches. His age could not have been more than forty, and his countenance reminded one of the handsome Mahratta type, especially in the brilliancy of his keen black eyes; but it was difficult to trace the fine features of tne race, disfigured and pitted as they were by the marks of small-pox. He was in the prime of life, and his figure was robust and supple. A close observer would have seen that he had lost one finger of his left hand. His hair was dyed a red colour, and he went barefoot, wearing only a turban, and a scanty shirt or tunic of striped woollen stuff girded round his waist.

On his breast were represented in bright colours the emblems of the two principles of preservation and destruction taught by Hindoo mythology: the lion's head of the fourth incarnation of Vishnu, the three eyes and the symbolic trident of the ferocious Siva.

There was great stir and commotion that evening in the streets of Aurungabad, especially in the lower quarters, where the populace swarmed outside the hovels in which they lived. Men, women, children, Europeans and natives; English soldiers, sepoys, beggars of all descriptions; peasants from the villages, met, talked, gesticulated, discussed the proclamation, and calculated the chances of winning the enormous reward offered by Government. The excitement was as great as it could have been before the wheel of a lottery where the prize was 2000*l*. In this case the fortunate ticket was the head of Dandou Pant, and to obtain it a man must first have the good luck to fall in with the Nabob, and then the courage to seize him.

The fakir, apparently the only person unexcited by the hope of winning the prize, threaded his way among the eager groups, occasionally stopping and listening to what was said, as though he might hear something of use to him. He spoke to no one, but if his lips were silent his eyes and ears were on the alert.

"Two thousand pounds for finding the Nabob!" exclaimed one, raising his clenched hands to heaven.

"Not for finding him," replied another, "but for catching him, which is a very different thing!"

"Well, to be sure, he is not a man to let himself be taken without a resolute struggle."

"But surely it was said he died of fever in the jungles of Nepaul?"

"That story was quite untrue! The cunning fellow chose to pass for dead, that he might live in greater security!"

"The report was spread that he had been buried in the midst of his encampment on the frontier!"

"It was a false funeral, on purpose to deceive people."

The fakir did not change a muscle of his countenance on hearing this latter assertion, which was made in a tone admitting of no doubt. But when one of the more excited of the group near which he was standing began to relate the following circumstantial details, his brows knit involuntarily as he listened.

"It is very certain," said the speaker, "that in 1859 the Nabob took refuge with his brother, Balao Rao, and the ex-rajah of Gonda, Debi-Bux-Singh, in a camp at the foot of the mountains of Nepaul. There, finding themselves closely pressed by the British troops, they all three resolved to cross the Indo-Chinese frontier. Before doing so, they caused a report of their death to be circulated, in order to confirm which they went through the ceremony of actual funerals; but in fact only a finger from the left hand of each man had been really buried. These they cut off themselves when the rites were celebrated."

"How do you know all this?" demanded one of the crowd of listeners.

"I myself was present," answered the man. "The soldiers of Dandou Pant had taken me prisoner. I only effected my escape six months afterwards."

While the Hindoo was speaking, the fakir never took his gaze off him. His eyes blazed like lightning. He kept his left hand under the ragged folds of his garment, and his lips quivered as they parted over his sharp-pointed teeth.

"So you have seen the Nabob?" inquired one of the audience.

"I have," replied the former prisoner of Dandou Pant.

"And would know him for certain if accident were to bring you face to face with him?"

"Assuredly I would : I know him as well as I know myself."

"Then you have a good chance of gaining the 2000*l*. ! " returned his questioner, not without a touch of envy in his tone.

"Perhaps so," replied the Hindoo, "if it be true that the Nabob has been so imprudent as to venture into the presidency of Bombay, which to me appears very unlikely."

"What would be the reason of his venturing so far? What reason would induce him to dare so much?"

"No doubt he might hope to instigate a fresh rebellion, either among the sepoys or among the country populations of Central India."

"Since Government asserts that he is known to be in the province," said one of the speakers, who belonged to that class which takes for gospel everything stated by authority, "of course Government has reliable information on the subject."

"Be it so!" responded the Hindoo; "only let it be the will of Brahma that Dandou Pant crosses my path, and my fortune is made!"

The fakir withdrew a few paces, but he did not lose sight of the ex-prisoner of the Nabob.

It was by this time dark night-time, but there was no diminution of the commotion in the streets of Aurungabad.

Gossip about the Nabob circulated faster than ever. Here, people were saying that he had been seen in the town; there, that he was known to be at a great distance. A courier from the north was reported to have arrived, with news for the Governor, of his arrest. At nine o'clock the best informed asserted that he was already imprisoned in the town jail—in company with some Thugs who had been vegetating there for more than thirty years; that he was going to be hanged next day at sunrise without a trial, just like Tantia Topi, his celebrated comrade in revolt.

But by ten o'clock there was fresh news. The prisoner had escaped, and the hopes of those who coveted the reward revived.

In reality all these reports were false.

Those supposed to be the best informed knew no more than any one else. The Nabob's head was safe. The prize was still to be won.

It was evident that the Indian who was acquainted with the person of Dandou Pant had a better chance of gaining the reward than any one else. Very few people, especially in the presidency of Bombay, had had occasion to meet with the savage leader of the great insurrection.

Farther to the north, or more in the centre of the country —in Scinde, in Bundelkund, in Oude, near Agra, Delhi, Cawnpore, Lucknow, on the principal theatre of the atrocities committed by his order—the population would have risen in a body, and delivered him over to British justice.

The relatives of his victims—husbands, brothers, children, wives—still wept for those whom he had caused to be massacred by hundreds.

Ten years had passed, but had not extinguished the righteous sentiments of horror and vengeance. It seemed, therefore, impossible that Dandou Pant should be so imprudent as to trust himself in districts where his name was held in execration.

If, then, he really had, as was supposed, re-crossed the Indo-Chinese frontier—if some hidden motive, whether projects for new revolt or otherwise, had induced him to quit the secret asylum which had hitherto remained unknown even to the Anglo-Indian police—it was only in the provinces of the Deccan that he could expect an open course and a species of security.

And we have seen that the Governor had, in point of fact, got wind of his appearance in the presidency, and instantly a price had been set on his head.

Still it must be remarked that men of the upper ranks at Aurungabad—magistrates, military officers, and public functionaries—considerably doubted the truth of the information received by the Governor.

It had so often been reported that this man had been seen, and even captured! So much false intelligence had been circulated respecting him, that there began to be a kind of legendary belief in a gift of ubiquity possessed by him, to account for the skill with which he eluded the most able and active agents of the police. The population, however, made no doubt that the intelligence as to his appearance was reliable.

Among those now most convinced that the Nabob was to be found was, of course, his ex-prisoner.

The poor wretch, allured by the hope of gain, and likewise animated by a spirit of personal revenge, began to set about the undertaking at once, and regarded his success as almost certain.

His plan was very simple.

He proposed next day to offer his services to the Governor; then, after having learned exactly all that was known of Dandou Pant—that is to say, the particulars on which was founded the information referred to in the proclamation, he intended to make his way at once to the locality in which the Nabob was reported to have been seen.

About eleven o'clock at night the Indian began to think of retiring to take some repose. His only resting-place was a small boat moored by the banks of the Doudhma; and thither he directed his steps, his mind full of the various reports he had heard, as, with half-closed eyes and thoughtful brow, he revolved the project he had resolved to carry out.

Quite unknown to him the fakir dogged his steps; he followed noiselessly, and, keeping in the shadow, never for an instant lost sight of him.

Towards the outskirts of this quarter of Aurungabad the streets became gradually deserted. The chief thoroughfare opened upon bare, unoccupied ground, one circuit of which skirted the stream of the Doudhma. The place was a kind of desert beyond the town, though within its walls a few passengers were hastily traversing it, evidently anxious to reach more frequented paths. The footsteps of the last died away in the distance, but the Hindoo did not remark that he was now alone on the river's bank.

The fakir was at no great distance, but concealed by trees, or beneath the sombre walls of ruined habitations, which were scattered here and there.

His precautions were needful. When the moon rose and shed uncertain rays athwart the gloom, the Hindoo might have seen that he was watched, and even very closely followed.

As to hearing the sound of the fakir's tread, it was utterly impossible. Barefoot, he glided, rather than walked. Nothing revealed his presence on the banks of the Doudhma.

Five minutes passed. The Hindoo took his way mechanically towards his wretched boat, like a man accustomed to withdraw night after night to this desert place.

He was absorbed in the thought of the interview he meant to have next day with the Governor; while the hope of revenging himself on the Nabob—never remarkable for his tenderness towards his prisoners—united with a burning desire to obtain the reward, rendered him blind and deaf to everything around him; and though the fakir was gradually approaching him, he was totally unconscious of the danger in which his imprudent words had placed him.

Suddenly a man sprang upon him with a bound like that of a tiger! He seemed to grasp a lightning flash. It was the moonlight glancing on the blade of a Malay dagger!

The Hindoo, struck in the breast, fell heavily to the ground. The wound, inflicted by an unerring hand, was mortal; but a few inarticulate words escaped the unhappy man's lips, with a torrent of blood.

The assassin stooped, raised his victim, and supported him while he turned his own face to the full light of the moon.

"Dost know me?" he asked.

"It is he!" murmured the Indian; and the dreaded name would have been his last choking utterance, but his head fell back, and he expired.

In another instant the corpse had disappeared beneath the waters of the Doudhma.

The fakir waited until the noise of the plunge had passed away; then, turning swiftly, he traversed the open ground, and passing along the now deserted streets and lanes, approached one of the city gates.

This gate was closed for the night just before he reached it, and a military guard occupied the post, to prevent either ingress or egress. The fakir could not leave Aurungabad, as he had intended to do.

"Yet depart this night I must, if ever I am to do it alive!" muttered he.

He turned away, and followed the inner line of fortifications for some little distance; then, ascending the slope, reached the upper part of the rampart. The crest towered fifty feet above the level of the fosse which lay between the scarp and counterscarp, and was devoid of any salient points or projections which could have afforded support. It seemed quite impossible that any man could descend without a rope, and the cord he wore as a girdle was but a few feet in length.

He paused, glanced keenly round, and considered what was to be done.

Great trees rise within the walls of Aurungabad, which seems set in a verdant frame of foliage. The branches of these being long and flexible, it might be possible to cling to one, and at great risk, drop over the wall.

No sooner did this idea occur to the fakir, than, without a moment's hesitation, he plunged among the boughs, and soon reappeared outside the wall, holding a long pliable branch, which he grasped midway, and which gradually bent beneath his weight.

When the branch rested on the edge of the wall, the fakir began to let himself slowly downwards, as though he held a knotted rope in his hands. By this means he descended a considerable distance; but when close to the extremity of the bough, at least thirty feet still intervened between him and the ground. There he hung, swinging in the air by his outstretched arms, while his feet sought some crevice or rough stone for support.

A flash!—another! The report of musketry!

The sentries had perceived the fugitive and fired upon him. He was not hit, but a ball struck the branch which supported him, and splintered it.

In a few seconds it gave way, and down went the fakir into the fosse. Such a fearful fall would have killed another man—he was uninjured.

To spring to his feet, dart up the slope of the counterscarp amid a storm of bullets—not one of which touched him—and vanish in the darkness, was mere play to the agile fugitive.

At a distance of two miles he passed the cantonments of the English troops, quartered outside Aurungabad.

A couple of hundred paces beyond that he stopped, turned round, and stretching his mutilated hand towards the city, fiercely uttered these words:—

"Woe betide those who fall now into the power of Dandou Pant! Englishmen have not seen the last of Nana Sahib!"

Nana Sahib! This name, the most formidable to which the revolt of 1857 had given a horrid notoriety, was there once more, flung like a haughty challenge at the conquerors of India.

CHAPTER II.

COLONEL MUNRO.

"MAUCLER, my dear fellow, you tell us nothing about your journey!" said my friend Banks, the engineer, to me. "One would suppose you had never got beyond your native Paris! What do you think of India?"

"Think of India!" I replied. "I really must see it before I can answer that question!"

"Well, that is good!" returned Banks. "Why, you have just traversed the entire peninsula from Bombay to Calcutta, and unless you are downright blind—"

"I am not blind, my dear Banks; but during that journey you speak of I was blinded."

"Blinded?"

"Yes! quite blinded by smoke, steam, dust; and, above all, by the rapid motion. I don't want to speak evil of railroads, Banks, since it is your business to make them; but let me ask whether you call it travelling to be jammed up in the compartment of a carriage, see no further than the glass of the windows on each side of you, tear along day and night, now over viaducts among the eagles and vultures, now through tunnels among moles and rats, stopping only at stations one exactly like another, seeing nothing of towns but the outside of their walls and the tops of their minarets, and all this amid an uproar of snorting engines, shrieking steam-whistles, grinding and grating of rails, varied by the mournful groans of the brake? Can you, I say, call this travelling so as to see a country?"

"Well done!" cried Captain Hood. "There, Banks! answer that if you can. What is your opinion, colonel?"

The colonel, thus addressed, bent his head slightly, and merely said,—

"I am curious to know what reply Banks can make to our guest, Monsieur Maucler."

"I reply without the slightest hesitation," said the engineer, "that I quite agree with Maucler."

"But then," cried Captain Hood, "why do you construct these railroads at all?"

"To enable you to go from Calcutta to Bombay in sixty hours when you are in a hurry."

"I am never in a hurry."

"Ah, well then, you had better take to the great trunk road and walk!"

"That is exactly what I intend doing."

"When?"

"When the colonel will agree to accompany me in a pretty little stroll of eight or nine hundred miles across the country!"

The colonel smiled, and without speaking again fell into one of the long reveries from which his most intimate friends, among whom were Captain Hood and Banks the engineer, found it difficult to rouse him.

I had arrived in India a month previously, having journeyed by the Great Indian Peninsular Railway, which runs from Bombay to Calcutta, *vid* Allahabad. I knew literally nothing of the country.

But it was my purpose to travel through its northern districts beyond the Ganges, to visit its great cities, to examine and study the principal monuments of antiquity, and to devote to my explorations sufficient time to render them complete.

I had become acquainted with the engineer Banks in Paris. For some years we had been united by a friendship which only increased with greater intimacy. I had promised to visit him at Calcutta as soon as the completion of that part of the Scinde, Punjab, and Delhi railroad, of which he was engineer, should set him at liberty.

The works being now at an end, Banks had some months leave, and I had come to propose that he should take rest by roaming over India with me! As a matter of course he had accepted my proposal with enthusiasm, and in a few weeks, when the season would be favourable, we were to set off.

On my arrival at Calcutta in the month of March, 1867, Banks had introduced me to one of his gallant comrades, Captain Hood, and afterwards to his friend Colonel Munro, at whose house we were spending the evening.

The colonel, at this time a man of about forty-seven, occupied a house in the European quarter; it stood somewhat apart, and consequently beyond the noise and stir of the great metropolis of India, which consists in fact of two cities, one native, the other foreign and commercial.

This English quarter is sometimes called "the city of palaces," and certainly it abounds with palaces if the name is to be applied to every building which can boast of porticoes and terraces. Calcutta is a rendezvous for all the orders of architecture which English taste lays under contribution when constructing her colonial capitals.

As to the residence of Colonel Munro, it was a simple "bungalow," a dwelling of one story raised on a brick basement, and having a pointed pyramidal roof. It was surrounded by a verandah supported on light columns. The kitchens, offices, coach-house, stables, and out-houses, formed two wings. A garden shaded by fine trees, and bounded by a low wall, enclosed the whole.

The colonel's house was evidently that of a man in easy circumstances. There was a large staff of servants, such as is required in Anglo-Indian families. The furniture and every household arrangement was in the very best taste and style. In everything about the establishment might be traced the hand of an intelligent woman, whose thoughtful care must have originally planned the comforts and conveniences of the home, but at the same time one felt that this woman was there no longer.

The management of the household was conducted entirely by an old soldier of the colonel's regiment, who acted as his steward or major-domo. Sergeant McNeil was a Scotchman, who had been with him in many campaigns, not merely in his military capacity, but as an attached and devoted personal attendant.

He was a man of five-and-forty or thereabouts, of tall and vigorous frame, and manly, well-bearded countenance. Although he had retired from the service when his colonel did, he continued to wear the uniform; and this national costume, together with his martial bearing, bespoke him at once the Highlander and the soldier.

Both had left the army in 1860. But instead of returning to the hills and glens of their native land, both had remained in India, and lived at Calcutta in a species of retirement and solitude, which requires to be explained.

When my friend Banks was about to introduce me to Colonel Munro, he gave me one piece of advice.

"Make no allusion to the sepoy revolt," he said: "and, above all, never mention the name of Nana Sahib."

Colonel Edward Munro belonged to an old Scottish family, whose members had made their mark in the history of former days.

He was descended from that Sir Hector Munro who in 1760 commanded the army in Bengal, when a serious insurrection had to be quelled. This he effected with a stern and pitiless energy. In one day twenty-eight rebels were blown from the cannon's mouth—a fearful sentence, many times afterwards carried out during the mutiny of 1857.

At the period of that great revolt Colonel Munro was in command of the 93rd Regiment of Highlanders, which he led during the campaign under Sir James Outram— one of the heroes of that war—of whom Sir Charles Napier spoke as "The Chevalier Bayard of the Indian Army." Colonel Munro was with him at Cawnpore; and also, in the second campaign, he was at the siege of Lucknow, and continued with Sir James until the latter was appointed a Member of the Council of India at Calcutta.

In 1858 Colonel Munro was made a Knight Commander of the Star of India, and was created a baronet. His beloved wife never bore the title of Lady Munro, for she perished at Cawnpore on the 27th June, 1857, in the atrocious massacre perpetrated by the orders and before the eyes of Nana Sahib.

COLONEL MUNRO.

Lady Munro (her friends always called her so) had been perfectly adored by her husband. She was scarcely seven-and-twenty at the time of her terrible death. Mrs. Orr and Miss Jackson, after the taking of Lucknow, were miraculously saved and restored to their husband and father. But to Colonel Munro nothing remained of his wife. She had disappeared with the two hundred victims in the well of Cawnpore.

Sir Edward, now a desperate man, had but one object remaining in life; it was to quench a burning thirst for vengeance—for justice. The discovery of Nana Sahib, for whom, by order of Government, search was being made in all directions, was his one great desire, his sole aim.

It was in order to be free to prosecute this search that he had retired from the army.

Sergeant McNeil got his discharge at the same time, and faithfully followed his master. The two men were animated by one hope, lived in one thought, had but one end in view; and eagerly starting in pursuit, followed up one track after another, only to fail as completely as the Anglo-Indian police had done. The Nana escaped all their efforts.

After three years spent in fruitless attempts, the colonel and Sergeant McNeil suspended their exertions for a time.

Just then the report of Nana Sahib's death was current in India, and this time it seemed to be so well attested as to admit of no reasonable doubt.

Sir Edward Munro and McNeil returned to Calcutta, and established themselves in the lonely bungalow which has been described. There the colonel lived in retirement, never left home, read nothing which could contain any reference to the sanguinary time of the mutiny, and seemed to live but for the cherished memory of his wife. Time in no way mitigated his grief.

I learned these particulars from my friend Banks, on our way to the house of mourning, as Sir Edward's bungalow might be called. It was very evident why he had warned me against making any allusion to the sepoy revolt and its cruel chief.

It must be noted that a report of Nana's reappearance in Bombay, which had for some days been circulating, had not reached him. Had it done so, he would have been on the move at once.

Banks and Captain Hood were tried friends of the colonel's, and they were his only constant visitors.

The former, as I have said, had recently completed the works he had in charge, on the Great Indian Peninsular Railway. He was a man in the prime of life, and was now appointed to take an active part in constructing the Madras Railway, designed to connect the Arabian Sea with the Bay of Bengal, but which was not to be commenced for a year. He was just now on leave at Calcutta, occupied with many mechanical projects, for his mind was active and fertile, incessantly devising some novel invention. His spare time he devoted to the colonel, whose fast friend he had been for twenty years. Thus most of his evenings were spent in the verandah of the bungalow. There he usually met Captain Hood, who belonged to the 1st squadron of Carabineers, and had served in the campaign of 1857-58 first under Sir John Campbell in Oude and Rohilcunde, and afterwards in Central India, under Sir Hugh Rose, during the campaign which terminated in the taking of Gwalior.

Hood was not more than thirty; he had spent most of his life in India, and was a distinguished member of the Madras Club. His hair and beard were auburn, and he belonged to an English regiment; otherwise he was thoroughly "Indianised," and loved the country as if it had been his by birth. He thought India the only place worth living in. And there, certainly, all his tastes were gratified. A soldier by nature and temperament, opportunities for fighting were of constant recurrence. An enthusiastic sportsman, was he not in a land where nature had collected together all the wild animals in creation, all the furred and feathered game of either hemisphere? A determined mountaineer, the magnificent ranges of Thibet offered him the ascent of the loftiest summits on the globe.

An intrepid traveller, what debarred him from setting foot on the hitherto untrodden regions of the Himalayan frontier? Madly fond of horse-racing, the race-courses of India appeared to him fully as important as those of Newmarket or Epsom.

On this latter subject Banks and Hood were quite at variance. The engineer took very little interest in the turfy triumphs of "Gladiator," and Co.

One day, when Hood had been urging him to express some opinion on the point, Banks said that to his mind races could never be really exciting but on one condition.

"And what is that?" demanded Hood.

"It should be clearly understood," returned Banks quite seriously, "that the jockey last at the winning-post is to be shot in his saddle."

"Ah! not a bad idea!" exclaimed Hood, very simply. Nor would he have hesitated to run the chance himself.

Such were Sir Edward Munro's two constant visitors, and without joining in their conversations he liked to listen to them. Their perpetual discussions and disputes, on all sorts of subjects, often brought a smile to his lips.

One wish and desire these two brave fellows had in common. And that was to induce the colonel to join them in making a journey, and so to vary the melancholy tenour of his thoughts. Several times they had tried to persuade him to go to places frequented during the hot season by the rich dwellers in Calcutta.

The colonel was immovable.

He had heard of the journey which Banks and I proposed to take. This evening the subject was resumed. Captain Hood's idea was a vast walking-tour in the north of India. He objected to railroads, as Banks did to horses. The middle course proposed was to travel either in carriages or in palanquins—easy enough on the great thoroughfares of Hindoostan.

"Don't tell me about your bullock-waggons and your humped-zebu carriages!" cried Banks. "I believe if you had your way without us engineers, you would still go about in primitive vehicles such as were discarded in Europe 500 years ago."

"I'm sure they are far more comfortable than some of your contrivances, Banks. And think of those splendid white bullocks! why, they keep up a gallop admirably, and you find relays at every two leagues—"

"Yes; and they drag a machine on four wheels after them, in which one is tossed and pitched worse than in a boat at sea in a storm."

"Well, I can't say much for these conveyances, certainly," answered Hood. "But have we not capital carriages for two, three, or four horses, which in speed can rival some of your trains? For my part, give me a palanquin rather than a train."

"A palanquin, Hood! Call it a coffin—a bier—where you are laid out like a corpse!"

"That's all very well, but at least you are not rattled and shaken about. In a palanquin you may write, read, or sleep at your ease, without being roused up for your ticket at every station. A palanquin carried by four or six Bengalee gamals (bearers) will take you at the rate of four-and-a-half miles an hour, and ever so much safer, too, than your merciless express trains!"

"The best plan of all," said I, "would certainly be to carry one's house with one."

"Oh you snail!" cried Banks.

"My friend," replied I, "a snail who could leave his shell, and return to it at pleasure, would not be badly off. To travel in one's own house, a rolling house, will probably be the climax of inventions in the matter of journeying!"

"Perhaps it will," said Colonel Munro, who had not yet spoken. "If the scene could be changed without leaving home and all its associations, if the horizon, points of view, atmosphere, and climate could be varied while one's daily life went on as usual—yes, perhaps—"

"No more travellers' bungalows," said Hood, "where

comfort is unknown, although for stopping there you require a leave from the local magistrate."

"No more detestable inns, in which one is fleeced morally and physically!" said I.

"What a vision of delight!" cried Captain Hood. "Fancy stopping when you please, setting off when you feel inclined, going at a foot's pace when disposed to linger, racing away at a gallop the instant the humour strikes you! Then to carry with you not only a bedroom, but drawing, and dining, and smoking-rooms! and a kitchen! and a cook! That would be something like progress, indeed Banks! and a hundred times better than railways. Contradict me if you dare!"

"Far from contradicting, I should entirely agree with you, if only you carried your notion of improvement far enough."

"What? do you mean to say better still might be done?"

"Listen, and judge for yourself. You consider that a moving house would be superior to a carriage—to a saloon-carriage—even to a sleeping-car on a railroad. And supposing one travelled for pleasure only, and not on business, you are right; I suppose we are agreed as to that?"

"Yes," said I, "we all think so;" and Colonel Mu made a sign of acquiescence.

"Well," continued Banks. "Now let us proceed. You give your orders to your coach-builder and architect combined, who turns you out a perfect realization of the idea, and there you have your rolling house, answering in every way to your requirements, replete with every convenience and comfort; not so high as to make one fear a somersault, not so broad as to suggest the possibility of sticking in a narrow road; well hung—in short, perfection. Let us suppose it has been built for our friend Colonel Munro; he invites us to share his hospitality, and proposes to visit the northern parts of India—like snails if you please, but snails who are not glued by the tail to their shells. All is prepared—nothing forgotten, not even the precious cook and kitchen so dear to our friend Hood. The day for starting comes! All right! Holloa! who is to draw your house my good friend?"

"Draw it?" cried Hood; "why mules, asses, horses, bullocks!"

"In dozens?" said Banks.

"Ah! let's see; elephants, of course—elephants! It would be something superb, majestic, to see a house drawn by a team of elephants, well-matched, and with splendid action. Can you conceive a more lordly and magnificent style of progression? Would it not be glorious?"

"Well—yes—but—"

'But! still another of your 'buts.''

"And a very big 'but' it is."

"Bother your engineers! you are good for nothing but to discover difficulties."

"And to surmount them when insurmountable," replied Banks quietly.

"Well then, surmount this one."

"I will—and in this way. My dear Munro, Captain Hood offers us a large choice of motive power, but none which is incapable of fatigue, none which will not on occasion prove restive or obstinate, and above all, require to eat. It follows that the travelling house we speak of is quite impracticable unless it can be a steam house."

"And run upon rails, of course! I thought so!" cried the captain, shrugging his shoulders.

"No, upon roads," returned Banks; "drawn by a first-rate traction engine."

"Bravo!" shouted Hood, "bravo! Provided the house need not follow your imperious lines of rails, I agree to the steam."

"But," said I to Banks, "an engine requires food as much as mules, asses, horses, bullocks, or elephants do, and for want of it will come to a standstill."

"A steam horse," replied he, "is equal in strength to several real horses, and the power may be indefinitely increased. The steam horse is subject neither to fatigue nor to sickness. In all latitudes, through all weathers, in sunshine, rain, or snow, he continues his unwearied course. He fears not the attack of wild beasts, the bite of serpents nor the stings of venomous insects. Desiring neither rest nor sleep, he needs no whip, spur, or goad. The steam horse, provided only he is not required at last to be cooked for dinner, is superior to every draught animal which Providence has placed at the disposal of mankind. All he consumes is a little oil or grease, a little coal or wood; and you know, my friends, that forests are not scarce in our Indian peninsula, and the wood belongs to everybody."

"Well said!" exclaimed Captain Hood. "Hurrah for the steam horse! I can almost fancy I see the travelling house, invented by Banks the great engineer, travelling the highways and byeways of India, penetrating jungles, plunging through forests, venturing even into the haunts of lions, tigers, bears, panthers, and leopards, while we, safe within its walls, are dealing destruction on all and sundry! Ah, Banks, it makes my mouth water! I wish I wasn't going to be born for another fifty years!"

"Why not, my dear fellow?"

"Because fifty years hence your dream will come true; we shall have the steam house."

"It is ready now," said Banks simply.

"Ready! Who has made one? Have you?"

"I have; and to tell you the truth, I rather expect it will even surpass your visionary hopes."

"My dear Banks, let's be off at once!" cried Hood, as if he had received an electric shock.

The engineer begged him to be calm, and turning to Sir Edward Munro, addressed him in an earnest tone.

"Edward," said he, "if I place a steam house at your command—if a month hence, when the season will be suitable, I come and tell you that your rooms are prepared, and that you can occupy them and go wherever you like, while your friends Maucler, Hood, and I are ready and willing to accompany you on an excursion to the north of India—will you answer me, 'Let us start, Banks, let us start ; and the God of the traveller be our speed'?"

"Yes, my friends," replied Colonel Munro, after a few moments' reflection. "Yes, I agree. I place at your disposal, Banks, the requisite funds. Keep your promise. Bring to us this ideal of a steam house, which is to surpass even Hood's imagination, and we will travel over all India."

"Hurrah! hurrah! hurrah!" shouted Captain Hood. "Now for wild sports on the frontiers of Nepaul!"

At this moment Sergeant McNeil, attracted by the captain's ringing cheers, appeared at the entrance to the verandah.

"McNeil," said Colonel Munro, "we start in a month for the north of India. Will you go?"

"Certainly, colonel, if you do," he replied.

CHAPTER III.

THE SEPOY REVOLT.

SOME account must now be given of the state of India at the period when the events of this story took place, and especially it will be necessary to relate the chief circumstances connected with the formidable revolt of the sepoys.

The Honourable East India Company, called sometimes by the nickname of "John Company," was founded in 1600, in the reign of Elizabeth, in the midst of a population of two hundred millions, inhabiting the sacred land of Aryavarta.

Their first title was merely "The Governor and Company of Merchants of London trading to the East Indies," and at their head was placed the Duke of Cumberland.

About this time the power of the Portuguese, which till then had been very great in the Indies, began to diminish. Of this the English immediately took advantage, and made their first attempt at a political and military administration in the presidency of Bengal ; its capital, Calcutta, to be the centre of the new government.

A French Company was founded about the same period, under the patronage of Colbert, and the conflicting interests of the rival companies gave rise to endless contentions, in which, a century later, the names of Dupleix, Labourdonnais, and Count de Lally, are distinguished both in successes and reverses.

The French were finally compelled to abandon the Carnatic, that portion of the peninsula which comprehends a part of its eastern coast.

Lord Clive's brilliant successes having assured the English power in Bengal, Warren Hastings consolidated the empire Clive had founded, and from that time war and conquest went on, till England became master of that vast empire which has been described as "not less splendid and more durable than that of Alexander."

The Company, however, till then all powerful, began to lose its authority, and in 1784 a bill was passed placing it under the control of Government. In 1813 it lost the monopoly of trading to India, and in 1833 the right of trading to China.

Since the establishment of a military force in India, the army had always been composed of two distinct contingents, European and native. The first consisted of British cavalry and infantry regiments, and European infantry in service of the Company; the second, of native regulars, commanded by English officers. There was also artillery, which belonged to the Company, and was European with the exception of a few batteries.

When Lord William Bentinck was made Governor of Madras, he introduced some reforms which highly offended the native troops. The sepoys were required to clip their moustachios, shave their chins, and were forbidden to wear their marks of caste. A new regulation turban was also ordered for them. Incited by the sons of Tippoo Sahib, this was made the excuse for an outbreak, in which the garrison at Vellore rose against and massacred their officers and about a hundred English soldiers, even the sick in the hospital being butchered.

The English troops quartered at Arcot fortunately arrived in time to stem that rebellion.

This, however, showed that a slight cause would at any moment set the natives against their conquerors, and in 1857 imminent peril threatened our Eastern Empire.

The Mohammedans of both sects longed to set themselves free from the British yoke, but could not hope to do so while the Hindoo soldiery remained true to their salt. Unhappily the spark that was needed to inflame their passions was not long in being supplied. A suspicion had seized the Hindoo mind that their religion and caste were in danger; that the English had determined that all the natives should become Christians. They believed that the cartridges for their new Enfield rifles were purposely greased with pig's fat, so that when they bit off the ends they would be defiled, lose caste, and be compelled to embrace the Christian religion.

Now, in a country where the population renounces even the use of soap, because the fat of either a sacred or unclean animal may enter into its composition, it was found very difficult to enforce the use of cartridges prepared with this substance, especially as they had to be touched with the lips. The Government yielded in some degree to the outcry which was made; but it was quite in vain to modify the drill with the rifles, or to assert that the fats in question took no part in the manufacture of the cartridges. Not a sepoy in the army could be reassured or persuaded to the contrary.

At this time Lord Canning was at the head of the administration as governor-general. Perhaps this statesman deluded himself as to the extent of the movement. For some years past the star of the united kingdom had been growing visibly dimmer in the Hindoo sky. In 1842 the retreat from Cabul had diminished the prestige of the European conquerors. The attitude of the English army during the Crimean war had not in some instances been such as to sustain its military reputation. The sepoys, therefore, who were well acquainted with all that was happening on the shores of the Black Sea, thought the time had come when a revolt of the native troops would probably be successful. Their minds, already well prepared, were inflamed and excited by the bards, brahmins, and moulvis, who stirred them up by songs and exhortations.

At the beginning of the year 1857, whilst the contingent of the British army was reduced owing to exterior complications, Nana Sahib, otherwise called Dandou Pant, who had been residing near Cawnpore, had gone to Delhi, and twice to Lucknow, no doubt with the object of provoking the rising, prepared so long ago, for, in fact, very shortly after the departure of the Nana, the insurrection was declared.

On the 24th of February, at Berampore, the 34th regiment refused the cartridges. In the middle of the month of March an adjutant was massacred, and the regiment being disbanded after the punishment of the assassins, carried into the neighbouring provinces most active elements of revolt.

On the 10th of May, at Meerut, a little to the north of Delhi, the 3rd, 11th, and 20th regiments mutinied, killed their colonels and several staff officers, gave up the town to pillage, and then fell back on Delhi. Here the rajah, a descendant of Timour, joined them. The arsenal fell into their power, and the officers of the 54th regiment were slaughtered. On the 11th of May, at Delhi, Major Fraser and his officers were pitilessly massacred by the mutineers of Mirut, in the very palace of the European commandant; and on the 16th of May forty-nine prisoners, men, women, and children, fell under the hatchets of the assassins. On the 20th of May, the 26th regiment, cantonned near Lahore, killed the commandant of the fort and the European sergeant-major.

The impulse once given to these frightful butcheries, it was impossible to stop them.

On the 28th of May, at Nourabad, many Anglo-Indian officers fell victims.

The brigadier commandant, with his aide-de-camp, and many other officers, were murdered in the cantonments of Lucknow on the 30th of May.

On the 31st of May, at Bareilly, in the Rohilkund, several officers were surprised and massacred, without having time to defend themselves.

At Shahjahanpore, on the same date, were assassinated the collector and a number of officers by the sepoys of the 38th regiment; and the next day, beyond Barwar, many officers, women, and children, who were *en route* for the station of Sivapore, a mile from Aurungabad, fell victims.

In the first days of June, at Bhopal, were massacred a part of the European population; and at Jansi, under the inspiration of the terrible dispossessed Rani, all the women and children who took refuge in the fort were slaughtered with unexampled refinement of cruelty.

At Allahabad, on the 6th June, eight young ensigns fell by the sepoys' hands.

On the 14th of June, two native regiments revolted at Gwalior, and assassinated their officers.

On the 27th of June, at Cawnpore, expired the first hecatomb of victims, of every age and sex, all shot or drowned—a prelude to the fearful drama which was to take place there a few weeks later.

On the 1st of July, at Holkar, thirty-four Europeans—officers, women, and children—were massacred, and the town pillaged and burnt; and on the same day, at Ugow, the colonel and adjutant of the 23rd regiment were slain.

The second massacre at Cawnpore was on the 15th of July. On that day several hundred women and children—amongst them Lady Munro—were butchered with unequalled cruelty by the order of Nana himself, who called to his aid the Mussulmen butchers from the slaughter-houses. This atrocious act, and how the bodies were afterwards thrown down a well, is too well known to need further description.

On the 26th of September, in Lucknow, many were half cut to pieces, and then thrown still living into the flames.

Besides these, in all the towns, and throughout the whole country, there were isolated murders, which altogether gave to this mutiny a horrible character of atrocity.

To these butcheries the English generals soon replied by reprisals—necessary, no doubt, since they did much to inspire terror of the British name among the insurgents—but which were truly frightful.

At the beginning of the insurrection, at Lahore, Chief Justice Montgomery and Brigadier Corbett had managed to disarm, without bloodshed, the 8th, 16th, 26th, and 49th native regiments. At Moultan the 62nd and 29th regiments were also forced to surrender their arms, without being able to attempt any serious resistance. The same thing was done at Peshawar, to the 24th, 27th, and 51st regiments, who were disarmed by Brigadier S. Colton and Colonel Nicholson, just as the rebellion was about to burst. But the officers of the 51st regiment having fled to the mountains, a price was set on their heads, and all were soon brought back by the hill-men.

This was the beginning of the reprisals.

A column, commanded by Colonel Nicholson, attacked a native regiment, which was marching towards Delhi. The mutineers were soon defeated and dispersed, and 120 prisoners brought to Peshawar. All were indiscriminately condemned to death; but one out of three only were really executed. Ten cannon were placed on the drilling-ground, a prisoner fastened to each of their mouths, and five times were the ten guns fired, covering the plain with mutilated remains, in the midst of air tainted with the smell of burning flesh.

These men, as M. de Valbezen says in his book called "Nouvelles Études sur les Anglais et l'Inde," nearly all died with that heroic indifference which Indians know so well how to preserve even in the very face of death. "No need to bind me, captain," said a fine young sepoy, twenty years of age, to one of the officers present at the execution; and as he spoke he carelessly stroked the instrument of death. "No need to bind me; I have no wish to run away."

Such was the first and horrible execution, which was to be followed by so many others.

At the same time Brigadier Chamberlain published the following order to the native troops at Lahore, after the execution of two sepoys of the 55th regiment:—

"You have just seen two of your comrades bound to the cannon's mouth and blown to pieces; this will be the punishment of all traitors. Your conscience will tell you what penalties they will undergo in the other world. These two soldiers have been shot rather than hung on the gallows, because I wished to spare them the pollution of the executioner's touch, and prove thus that the Government, even at this crisis, wishes to avoid everything that would do the least injury to your prejudices of religion and caste."

On the 30th of July, 1237 prisoners fell successively before firing platoons, and fifty others only escaped to die of hunger and suffocation in the prisons in which they were shut up.

On the 28th of August, of 870 sepoys who fled from Lahore, 659 were pitilessly massacred by the soldiers of the British army.

After the taking of Delhi, on the 23rd of September, three princes of the king's family, the heir presumptive and his two cousins, surrendered unconditionally to Major Hodson, who brought them, with an escort of five men only, into the midst of a menacing crowd of 5000 Hindoos—one against 1000. And yet, half way through, Hodson stopped the cart which contained his prisoners, got into it, ordered them to lay bare their breasts, and then shot them all three with his revolver. "This bloody execution, by the hand of an English officer," says M. de Valbezen, "excited the highest admiration throughout the Punjab."

After the capture of Delhi, 3000 prisoners perished by shot or on the gallows, and with them twenty-nine members of the royal family. The siege of Delhi, it is true, had cost the besiegers 2151 Europeans, and 1686 natives.

At Allahabad horrible slaughter was made, not among

the sepoys, but in the ranks of the humble population, whom the fanatics had almost unconsciously enticed to pillage.

At Lucknow, on the 16th of November, 2000 sepoys were shot at the Sikander Bagh, and a space of 120 square yards was strewed with their dead bodies.

At Cawnpore, after the massacre, Colonel Neil obliged the condemned men, before giving them over to the gallows, to lick and clean with their tongues, in proportion to their rank of caste, each spot of blood remaining in the house in which the victims had perished. To the Hindoos, this was preceding death with dishonour.

During the expedition into Central India executions were continual, and under the fire of musketry "walls of human flesh fell and perished on the earth!"

On the 9th of March, 1858, during the attack on the Yellow House, at the time of the second siege of Lucknow, after the decimation of the sepoys, it appears certain that one of these unfortunate men was roasted alive by the Sikhs, under the very eyes of the English officers![1]

On the 11th, the moats of the Begum's palace at Lucknow were filled with sepoys' bodies; for the English could not restrain the rage that possessed them.

In twelve days, 3000 natives were slain, either hung or

[1] The translators beg to say that they are not responsible for any of the facts or sentiments contained in this account of the mutiny.

shot, including among them 380 fugitives on the island of Hydaspes, who were escaping into Cashmere.

In short, without counting the sepoys who were killed under arms during this merciless repression—in which no prisoners were made—in the Punjab only not less than 628 natives were shot or bound to the cannon's mouth by order of the military authorities, 1370 by order of the civil authority, 386 hung by order of both.

At the beginning of the year 1859 it was estimated that more than 120,000 native officers and soldiers had perished, and more than 200,000 civilian natives, who paid with their lives for their participation—often doubtful—in this insurrection. Terrible reprisals these; and perhaps, on that occasion, Mr. Gladstone had some reason on his side when he protested so energetically against them in Parliament.

It was important, for the better understanding of our story, that the death-list on both sides should be given as above, to make the reader comprehend the unsatiated hatred which still remained in the hearts of the conquered, thirsting for vengeance, as well as in those of the conquerors, who, ten years afterwards, were still mourning the victims of Cawnpore and Lucknow.

As to the purely military facts of the campaign against the rebels, they comprised the following expeditions, which may be summarily mentioned.

To begin with, Sir John Lawrence lost his life in the first Punjab campaign.

Then came the siege of Delhi (that central point of the insurrection), reinforced by thousands of fugitives, and in which Mohammed Shah Bahadour was proclaimed Emperor of Hindoostan. "Finish up Delhi!" was the impatient order of the Governor-General in his last despatch to the Commander-in-chief; and the siege, begun on the night of the 13th of June, was ended on the 19th of September, after costing the lives of Generals Sir Harry Barnard and John Nicholson.

At the same time, after Nana Sahib had had himself declared Peishwar, and been crowned at the castle fort of Bhitoor, General Havelock effected his march on Cawnpore. He entered it the 17th of July, though too late to prevent the second massacre, or to seize the Nana, who managed to escape with 5000 men and forty pieces of cannon.

Havelock then undertook a first campaign in the kingdom of Oude, and on the 28th of July he crossed the Ganges with 1700 men and ten cannon only, and proceeded towards Lucknow.

Sir Colin Campbell and Major-General Sir James Outram now appeared on the scene. The siege of Lucknow lasted eighty-seven days, and during it Sir Henry Lawrence and General Havelock lost their lives. Then

THE SEPOY REVOLT. 47

Sir Colin Campbell, after having been obliged to retire on Cawnpore, of which he took definite possession, prepared for a second campaign.

During this time other tropos captured Mohir, a town of Central India, and made an expedition across the Mulwa, which established the British authority in that kingdom.

At the commencement of the year 1858 Campbell and Outram again marched on Lucknow, with four divisions of infantry, commanded by Major-Generals Sir James Outram and Sir Edward Lugard, and Brigadiers Walpole and Franks. Sir Hope Grant led the cavalry, while Wilson and Robert Napier had other commands, the army consisting of about 25,000 men, which were joined by the Maharajah of Nepaul with 12,000 Ghoorkas. But the rebel army numbered not less than 120,000 men, and the town of Lucknow contained from 700,000 to 800,000 inhabitants. The first attack was made on the 6th of March.

On the 16th, after a series of combats, in which Major Hodson fell, and Sir William Peel, captain of H.M.S. "Shannon," who was then commanding the Naval Brigade, was severely wounded,[2] the English got possession of that part of the town situated on the left bank of the Goomtee. Moos-a-bagh was cannonaded and captured by Sir James

---

[2] This gallant officer, when still weak from his wound, was after the taking of Lucknow seized with the small-pox, under which he succumbed.—Trans.

Outram and Sir Hope Grant on the 19th ; and on the 21st, after a fierce struggle, the English took final possession of the city.

In the month of April an expedition was made into Rohilkund, as a great number of the fugitive insurgents were there. Bareilly, the capital of that kingdom, was the first object of the English, who were not at the outset very fortunate, as they suffered a sort of defeat at Jugdespore. Here also Brigadier Adrian Hope was killed. But towards the end of the month Campbell arrived, retook Shahjahanpore; and on the 5th of May, attacking Bareilly, he seized it, without having been able to prevent the rebels evacuating it.

The Central India Field Force, under the command of Sir Hugh Rose, performed many gallant achievements. This general, in January, 1858, marched through the kingdom of Bhopal, and relieved the town of Saugor, on the 3rd of February, which had been closely besieged since July, 1857.

Ten days after he took the fort of Gurakota, forced the defiles of the Vindhya chain, crossed the Betwa, and arrived before Jhansi, defended by 11,000 rebels, under the command of the savage Amazon Ranee; invested this place on the 22nd of March, in the midst of intense heat, detached 2000 men from the besieging army to meet 20,000 men from Gwalior, led by the famous Tantia Topee, put this chief to the rout, and then assaulted the town on the 2nd of April, forced the walls, and seized the citadel, from which the Ranee managed to escape. On the 23rd of May the British advanced on Calpee, and occupied it. The Ranee and Tantia Topee having taken possession of Gwalior, Sir Hugh Rose advanced upon that place; an action took place at Morar on the 16th of June, and on the 19th another fierce contest, in which the rebels were completely put to the rout, and the Central India Field Force returned to Bombay in triumph.

The Ranee was killed in a hand to hand fight before Gwalior. This famous queen, who was devoted to the Nabob, and was his most faithful companion during the insurrection, fell by the hand of Sir Edward Munro. Nana Sahib, by the dead body of Lady Munro at Cawnpore, the colonel, by the dead body of the Ranee at Gwalior, represent the revolt and the suppression, and were thus made enemies whose hatred would find terrible vent if they ever met face to face!

The insurrection might now be considered to be quelled, except in a few places in the kingdom of Oude. Campbell resumed the campaign on the 2nd of November, seized the last of the rebel places, and compelled several important chiefs to submit themselves. One of them however, Beni Madho, was not taken. In December was learnt that he had taken refuge in a neighbou district of Nepaul. It was said that Nana Sahib, Balao Rao his brother, and the Begum of Oude, were with him. Later it was reported that they had sought refuge across the Raptee, on the boundaries of the kingdoms of Nepaul and Oude. Campbell pressed rapidly on, but they had crossed the frontier. In the beginning of February, 1859, an English brigade, one of the regiments being under command of Colonel Munro, pursued them into Nepaul. Beni Madho was killed, the Begum of Oude and her son were made prisoners, and obtained permission to reside in the capital of Nepaul. As to Nana Sahib and Balao Rao, though for long they were thought to be dead, yet such was not the case.

Thus the terrible insurrection was crushed. Tantia Topee, betrayed by his lieutenant Man-Singh, and condemned to death, was executed on the 15th of April, at Sipree. This rebel, "this truly remarkable actor in the great drama of the Indian insurrection," says M. de Valbezen, "and one who gave proofs of a political genius full of resources and daring," died courageously on the scaffold.

This sepoy mutiny, which might perhaps have lost India to the English if it had extended all over the peninsula, and especially if the rising had been national, caused the downfall of the Honourable East India Company.

On the 1st of November, 1858, a proclamation, published in twenty languages, announced that Victoria, Queen of England, would wield the sceptre of India—that country of which, some years later, she was to be crowned Empress.

The governor, now called Viceroy, a Secretary of State, and fifteen members, composed the supreme government. The governors of the presidencies of Madras and Bombay were henceforward to be nominated by the Queen. The members of the Indian service and the commanders-in-chief to be chosen by the Secretary of State. Such were the principal arrangements of the new government.

As to the military force, the English army now contains seventeen thousand more men than before the sepoy mutiny. The army in 1876-7 numbered 64,902 European officers and men, and 125,246 native.

Such is the actual state of the peninsula from an administrative and military point of view; such the effective force which guards a territory of 400,000 square miles.

"The English," says M. Grandidier, "have been fortunate in finding in this large and magnificent country a gentle, industrious, and civilized people, who for long have been accustomed to a yoke. But they must be careful; gentleness has its limits, and the yoke should not be allowed to bruise their necks, or they may one day rebel and cast it off."

CHAPTER IV.

DEEP IN THE CAVES OF ELLORA.

IT was but too true. The Mahratta prince, Dandou Pant, adopted son of Baji Rao, Peishwar of Poona, known as Nana Sahib, and perhaps at this period the sole survivor of the leaders in the great insurrection, had dared to leave his inaccessible retreats amid the mountains of Nepaul. Full of courage and audacity, accustomed to face danger, crafty and skilled in the art of baffling and eluding pursuit in every form, he had ventured forth into the provinces of the Deccan, animated by hatred intensified a hundredfold since the terrible reprisals taken after the rebellion.

Yes; Nana Sahib had sworn deadly hate to the possessors of India.

Was he not the heir of Baji Rao? and when the Peishwar died in 1851, had not the Company refused to continue to pay to him his pension of eight lacs of rupees? This had been one of the causes of an enmity from which resulted the greater excesses.

But what could Nana Sahib hope for now?

The revolt had been completely quelled eight years before. The Honourable East India Company had gradually been superseded by the English Government, which now held the entire peninsula under an authority very much firmer and better established than that of the old mercantile associations.

Not a trace of the mutiny remained, for the ranks of the native regiments had been wholly reorganized.

Could the Nana dream of success in an attempt to foment a national movement among the lowest classes of Hindoostan? We shall see.

He was aware that his presence in the province of Aurungabad had been observed, that the governor and viceroy were informed of it, and that a price was set on his head. It was clear that precipitate flight was necessary, and that his place of refuge must be well concealed indeed if he hoped to baffle the search of the agents of Anglo-Indian police.

The Nana did not waste an hour of the night between the 6th and 7th of March. He perfectly knew the country, and resolved to gain Ellora, twenty-five miles from Aurungabad, and there join one of his accomplices.

The night was very dark. The would-be fakir, satisfied that no one was in pursuit, took his way towards the mausoleum, erected at some distance from the city, in honour of the Mohammedan Sha-Soufi, a saint whose relics have a high medicinal reputation. All within the mausoleum, priests and pilgrims, slept profoundly, and the Nana passed on without being subjected to inconvenient questioning.

Dark as it was, he soon discerned, four leagues further northward, the block of granite on which is reared the impregnable fortress of Dowlatabad. Rising abruptly from the plain to the height of 240 feet, its vast outline could be traced against the sky. But Nana Sahib, with a glance of hatred, turned his gaze away from the place; for one of his ancestors, an emperor of the Deccan, had wished to establish his capital at the base of this stronghold. It would indeed have been an impregnable position, well suited to be the central point of an insurrectionary movement in this part of India.

Having traversed the plain, a region of more varied and broken ground succeeded; the undulations gave notice of mountains in the distance. But the Nana did not slacken his pace, although often making steep ascents. Twenty-five miles, the distance that is between Ellora and Arungabad, had to be got over during the night; nothing therefore induced him to make a halt, although an open caravanserai lay near his path, and he passed a lonely and half-ruined bungalow among the hills, where he might have sought an hour's repose.

When the sun rose he was beyond the village of Ranzah,

which possesses the tomb of Arungzeeb, the most famous of Mogul emperors.

At length he had reached the celebrated group of excavations which take their name from the little neighbouring village of Ellora.

The hill in which these caves, to the number of thirty, have been hollowed out, is crescent-shaped. The monuments consist of twenty-four Buddhist monasteries and some grottoes of less importance. The basaltic quarry has been extensively worked by the hand of man. But the native architects, who, from the earliest ages extracted stones from it, had not for their main object the erection of the marvellous buildings here and there to be seen on the surface of the vast peninsula. No; they removed these stones in order to procure space within the living rock—space to be converted into "chaityas" or "viharas," as the case might be.

Among these temples, the most extraordinary is that of the Kaïlas. Let any one picture to himself an isolated block 120 feet in height by 600 in circumference. This block, with a bold audacity almost incredible, has been hewn out of the heart of the basaltic rock, and isolated in a space or court 360 feet long by 186 wide.

The block, thus detached, has been cut and carved by those wondrous architects as a sculptor might carve a piece of ivory. On the outside they have scooped columns, fashioned pyramids, rounded cupolas, reserving masses of rock where needed to throw out bas-reliefs, in which colossal elephants seem to sustain the entire edifice. Within, they have hollowed a vast hall surrounded by recesses or chapels, the vaulted roof resting on the detached columns of the entire mass. In short, out of this monolith they have made a temple, not "built" in the ordinary sense of the word—a temple unique in the world, worthy to rival the most marvellous edifices of India, and which cannot even lose in comparison with the marvels of Egypt.

This temple, now almost abandoned, has already been touched by the hand of Time. In some parts it shows signs of decay. It is only a thousand years old, but that which is early youth in the works of nature is already advanced age in those of man.

The arrival of Nana Sahib at Ellora was unobserved; he entered the caves and glided into one of several deep cracks or crevices which had opened in the basement, but were concealed behind the supporting elephants.

This opening admitted him into a gloomy passage or drain which ran beneath the temple, terminating in a sort of crypt or vaulted reservoir now dry and empty.

Advancing a short way into the passage, the Nana uttered a peculiar whistle, to which a sound precisely similar immediately replied; and a light flashed through the darkness, proving that the answer was no mocking echo.

Then an Indian appeared carrying a small lantern.

"Away with the light!" said the Nana.

"Dandou Pant!" said the Indian, extinguishing the lamp; "is it thou thyself?"

"My brother, it is I myself."

"Art thou—?"

"Let me eat first," returned the Nana; "we will converse afterwards. But let both eating and speaking be in darkness. Take my hand and guide me."

The Indian took his hand and drew him into the crypt, and he assisted him to lie down on a heap of withered grass and leaves, where he himself had been sleeping when roused by the fakir's signal.

The man, accustomed to move in the obscurity of this dismal retreat, soon produced food, consisting of bread, flesh of fowls prepared in a way common in India, and a gourd containing half a pint of the strong spirit known "arrack," distilled from the sap of the cocoanut-tree.

The Nana ate and drank, but spoke never a word. was faint and sinking through hunger and fatigue, and his whole vitality seemed concentrated in his eyes, which burned and flashed in the darkness like those of a tiger.

The Indian remained motionless, waiting till the Nabob chose to speak.

This man was Balao Rao, the brother of Nana Sahib. Balao Rao, a year older than Dandou Pant, resembled him physically, and might easily be mistaken for him. Morally the likeness was still more complete. In detestation of the English, in craft to form plots, and in cruelty to execute them, they were as one soul in two bodies. Throughout the rebellion these two brothers had kept together. After it was subdued, they shared together a refuge on the frontiers of Nepaul. And now, united by the single aim of resuming the struggle, they were both ready for action.

When the Nana had devoured the food set before him, he remained for some time leaning his head on his folded arms. Baloa Rao kept silence, thinking he wished to sleep.

But Dandou Pant raised his head suddenly, and grasping his brother's hand, said in a hollow voice, "I am denounced! There is a price set on my head! 2000*l*. promised to the man who delivers up Nana Sahib!"

"Thy head is worth more than that, Dandou Pant!" cried Balao Rao; "2000*l*. is hardly enough even for mine. They would be fortunate if they got the two for 20,000*l*."

"Yes," returned the Nana; "in three months, on the 23rd of June, will be the anniversary of the battle of Plassy. "Our prophets foretold that its hundredth anniversary, in 1857, should witness the downfall of British rule, and the emancipation of the children of the sun. Nine years more than the hundred have now all but passed, and

India still lies crushed and trodden beneath the invader's heel."

"That effort which failed in 1857 may and ought to succeed ten years afterwards," replied Balao Rao. "In 1827, '37 and '47, there were risings in India. The fever of revolt has broken out every ten years. Well—this year it will be cured by a bath of European blood!"

"Let but Brahma be our stay," murmured the Nana, "and then—life for life! Woe to the leaders of our foe who yet survive! Lawrence is gone, Barnard, Hope, Napier, Hodson, Havelock—all are gone. But Campbell, and Rose still live; and he whom, above all, I hate—that Colonel Munro, whose ancestor was the first to blow our men from the cannon's mouth, the man who with his own hand slew my friend the Ranee of Jansi. Let but that man fall into my power and he shall see whether I have forgotten the horrors of Colonel Neil, the massacres of Secunderabad, the slaughter in the Begum's palace, at Bareilly, Jansi, Morar, the island of Hydaspes, and at Delhi. He shall discover that I have sworn his death as he did mine."

"Has he not left the army?" inquired Balao Rao.

"He would re-enter the service the moment any disturbances broke out," replied Nana Sahib. "But even if our attempted rising were to fail, he should not escape, for I would stab him in his bungalow at Calcutta."

"So let it be—and now?"

"Now the work must begin. This time it shall be a national movement. Let but the Hindoos of towns, villages, and country places rise simultaneously, and very soon the sepoys will make common cause with them. I have traversed the centre and north of the Deccan; everywhere I have found minds ripe for revolt. We have leaders ready to act in every town and straggling village. The Brahmins will fanaticize the people. Religion this time will carry along with us the votaries of Siva and Vishnu. At the appointed time, at the given signal, millions of natives will rise, and the royal army will be annihilated!"

"And Dandou Pant?" exclaimed Balao Rao, seizing his brother's hand.

"Dandou Pant," continued the Nana, "will not only be the Peishwar crowned in the hill-fort of Bithour. He will be the sovereign of the whole sacred land of Hindoostan!"

Nana Sahib folded his arms, his abstracted look was that of a man whose mental eye is bent on the distant future, and he remained silent.

Balao Rao was careful not to rouse him. He loved to see the working of that fierce soul, burning as it were with a hidden fire, which he knew he could at any moment fan into a flame.

The Nana could not have had an accomplice more

devoted to his person, a counsellor more eager to urge him forward to attain his ends. He was to him, as has been said, a second self.

After a silence of some duration, the Nana raised his head—his thoughts had returned to the present.

"Where are our comrades?"

"In the caverns of Adjuntah, where they were appointed to wait for us."

"And our horses?"

"I left them a gunshot from this place, on the road between Ellora and Boregami."

"Is Kâlagani with them?"

"He is, my brother. They are rested, refreshed, and perfectly ready for us."

"Then let us start. We must be at Adjuntah before daybreak."

"And after that what must be done? Has not this enforced flight disarranged our previous plans?"

"No," replied Nana Sahib. "We must gain the heights of Sautpourra, where every defile is known to me, and where I can assuredly defy the pursuit of the English bloodhounds of police. There we shall be in the territory of the Bheels and Goonds who are faithful to our cause. There, in the midst of that mountainous region of the Vindhyas, where the standard of revolt may at any moment be raised, I shall await the favourable juncture!"

"Forward!" exclaimed Balao Rao, starting up, "and let those who want heads come and take them!"

"Yes—let them come," responded the Nana, grinding his teeth. "I am ready."

Balao Rao instantly made his way along the narrow passage which led to this dismal cell beneath the temple. On reaching the secret opening behind the colossal elephant, he cautiously emerged, looked anxiously on all sides amid the shadowy gloom, to ascertain that the coast was clear. Then advancing some twenty paces, and being satisfied that all was safe, he gave notice by a shrill whistle that the Nana might follow him.

Shortly afterwards the two brothers had quitted this artificial valley, the length of which is half a league, and which, sometimes to a great height, and in several stories, is pierced by galleries, vaulted chambers, and excavations. The distance between Ellora and Adjuntah is fifty miles, but the Nana was no longer the fugitive of Arungabad, travelling painfully on foot. Three horses awaited him, as his brother had said, under the care of his faithful servant Kâlagani. They were concealed in a thick forest about a mile from Ellora, and the three men were speedily mounted and galloping in the direction of Adjuntah. It was no strange thing to see a fakir on horseback. In point of fact, many of these impudent beggars demand alms from their seat in the saddle!

Although the time of the year was not that at which pilgrimages are usually made, yet the Nana avoided passing near the Mohammedan mausoleum frequented as a bungalow by pilgrims, travellers, and sightseers of all nations who often flock thither attracted by the wonders of Ellora, and pushed forward by a route as remote as possible from human habitations. He only halted occasionally to breathe the steeds, and to partake of the simple provisions which Kâlagani carried at his saddle-bow.

The ground was flat and level. In all directions stretched expanses of heath, crossed by massive ridges of dense jungle. But as they approached Adjuntah the country became more varied.

The superb grottoes or caves of Adjuntah, which rival those of Ellora, and perhaps in general beauty surpass them, occupy the lower end of a small valley about half a mile from the town. Nana Sahib could reach them without passing through it, and therefore felt himself secure, although so near a place where the governor's proclamation was fixed to every building.

Fifteen hours after quitting Ellora he and his two companions plunged into a narrow defile which led them into the celebrated valley where twenty-seven temples, hewn in the rocky wall, looked down into the giddy depths beneath.

It was night, superb though moonless, for the heavens glittered with starry constellations, when the Nana, Balao

Rao, and Kâlagani, approached their destination. Lofty trees and giant flowering plants stood out in strong relief against the sparkling sky. Not a breath stirred the air, not a leaf moved, not the faintest sound could be heard, save the dull murmur of a torrent which rolled in the depths of a ravine hundreds of feet below.

This murmur grew on the ear, however, and became a hoarse roar as the riders advanced to the cataract of Satkound, where the water, torn by sharp projections of quartz and basalt, plunges over a fall of fifty fathoms. As the travellers passed the chasm, a cloud of liquid dust whirled and eddied over it, which moonlight would have tinted with soft rainbow hues.

Here the defile made a sharp turn like an elbow, and the valley, in all its wealth of Buddhist architecture, lay before them.

On the walls of these temples—profusely adorned with columns, rose-tracery, arabesques, and galleries, peopled by colossal forms of grotesque animals, hollowed out into cells formerly occupied by the priests, who were the guardians of these sacred abodes—the artist may admire the bright colours of frescoes which seem as though painted but yesterday; frescoes which represent royal ceremonies, religious processions, and battles, exhibiting every weapon employed long before the Christian era in the great and glorious empire of India.

DEEP IN THE CAVES OF ELLORA. 65

To Nana Sahib all the secrets of these mysterious temples were well known. Already, more than once, he had, when closely pressed, sought refuge among them. The subterranean galleries connecting the temples, the narrow tunnels bored through solid walls of quartz, the winding passages crossing and recrossing in every direction, all the thousand ramifications of a labyrinth the clue to which might be sought in vain by the most patient, were familiar to him. Even with no torch to illumine their profound gloom, he was perfectly at home there.

Like a man sure of what he was about, the Nana made straight for one of the excavations less important than the rest. The entrance to it was filled up by a curtain of foliage and a mass of huge stones piled up in some ancient landslip, and thickly overgrown by shrubs and creepers.

The Nana gave notice of his presence at this concealed entrance simply by scraping his nail on a flat surface of stone.

Instantly the heads of two or three natives appeared among the branches; then ten, then twenty, showed themselves; and then soon, creeping and winding out like serpents from between the stones, came a party of forty well-armed men.

"Forward!" said Nana Sahib.

And seeking no explanation, ignorant of whither he led them, these faithful followers were ready to obey; and, if needful, lay down their lives for Dandou Pant. They were on foot, but could vie with the speed of any horse.

The little party made its way across the defile which skirted the abyss, keeping in a northerly direction, and rounding the shoulder of the hill. In an hour they reached the road to Kandeish, which finally leads to the passes of the Sautpourra mountains.

At daybreak they passed near the line of railway running from Bombay to Allahabad, above Nagpore.

On a sudden the Calcutta express dashed into sight, flinging masses of white vapour among the stately banyans, and startling with its shrieking whistle the wild inhabitants of the jungle.

The Nana drew bridle, and stretching his hand towards the flying train, exclaimed, in a strong stern voice,—

"Speed on thy way, and tell the Viceroy of India that Nana Sahib lives! Tell him that this railroad, the accursed work of the invaders' hands, shall ere long be drenched in their blood."

CHAPTER V

THE IRON GIANT.

On the morning of the 5th May, the passengers along the high road from Calcutta to Chandernagore, whether men women or children, English or native, were completely astounded by a sight which met their eyes. And certainly the surprise they testified was extremely natural.

At sunrise a strange and most remarkable equipage had been seen to issue from the suburbs of the Indian capital, attended by a dense crowd of people drawn by curiosity to watch its departure.

First, and apparently drawing the caravan, came a gigantic elephant. The monstrous animal, twenty feet in height, and thirty in length, advanced deliberately, steadily, and with a certain mystery of movement which struck the gazer with a thrill of awe. His trunk, curved like a cornucopia, was uplifted high in the air. His gilded tusks, projecting from behind the massive jaws, resembled a pair of huge scythes. On his back was a highly ornamented howdah, which looked like a tower surmounted, in Indian style, by a dome-shaped roof and furnished with lens-shaped glasses to serve for windows.

This elephant drew after him a train consisting of two enormous cars, or actual houses, moving bungalows in fact, each mounted on four wheels. The wheels, which were prodigiously strong, were carved, or rather sculptured, in every part. Their lowest portion only could be seen, as they moved inside a sort of case, like a paddle-box, which concealed the enormous locomotive apparatus. A flexible gangway connected the two carriages.

How could a single elephant, however strong, manage to drag these two enormous constructions, without any apparent effort? Yet this astonishing animal did so! His huge feet were raised and set down with mechanical regularity, and he changed his pace from a walk to a trot, without either the voice or a hand of a mahout being apparent.

The spectators were at first so astonished by all this, that they kept at a respectful distance; but when they ventured nearer, their surprise gave place to admiration.

They could hear a roar, very similar to the cry uttered by these giants of the Indian forests. Moreover, at intervals there issued from the trunk a jet of vapour.

And yet, it was an elephant!

The rugged greeny-black skin evidently covered the

bony framework of one that must be called the king of the pachydermes. His eyes were life-like; all his members were endowed with movement!

Ay! But if some inquisitive person had chanced to lay his hand on the animal, all would have been explained. It was but a marvellous deception, a gigantic imitation, having as nearly as possible every appearance of life.

In fact, this elephant was really encased in steel, and an actual steam-engine was concealed within its sides.

The train, or Steam House, to give it its most suitable name, was the travelling dwelling promised by the engineer.

The first carriage, or rather house, was the habitation of Colonel Munro, Captain Hood, Banks, and myself.

In the second lodged Sergeant McNeil and the servants of the expedition.

Banks had kept his promise, Colonel Munro had kept his; and that was the reason why, on this May morning, we were setting out in this extraordinary vehicle, with the intention of visiting the northern regions of the Indian peninsula.

But what was the good of this artificial elephant? Why have this fantastic apparatus, so unlike the usual practical inventions of the English? Till then, no one had ever thought of giving to a locomotive destined to travel either over macadam highways or iron rails, the shape and form of a quadruped.

I must say, the first time we were admitted to view the machine we were all lost in amazement. Questions about the why and wherefore fell thick and fast upon our friend Banks. We knew that this traction-engine had been constructed from his plans and under his directions. What, then, had given him the idea of hiding it within the iron sides of a mechanical elephant.

"My friends," answered Banks seriously, "do you know the Rajah of Bhootan?"

"I know him," replied Captain Hood, "or rather I did know him, for he died two months ago."

"Well, before dying," returned the engineer, "the Rajah of Bhootan not only lived, but lived differently to any one else. He loved pomp, and displayed it in every possible manner. He never denied himself anything—I mean anything that ever came into his head. His brain imagined the most impossible things, and had not his purse been inexhaustible, it would soon have been emptied in the process of gratifying all his desires. He was enormously rich, had coffers filled with lacs of rupees. Now one day an idea occurred to him, which took such possession of his mind as to keep him from sleeping—an idea which Solomon might have been proud of, and would certainly have realized, had he been acquainted with steam: this idea was to travel in a perfectly new fashion, and to have an equipage such as no one had before dreamt of. He knew me, and sent for me to his court, and himself drew the plan of his locomotive. If you imagine, my friends, that I burst into a laugh at the Rajah's proposition, you are mistaken. I perfectly understood that this grandiose idea sprung naturally from the brain of a Hindoo sovereign, and I had but one desire on the subject—to realize it as soon as possible, and in a way to satisfy both my poetic client and myself. A hardworking engineer hasn't an opportunity every day to exercise his talents in this fantastic way, and add an animal of this description to the creations of the 'Arabian Nights.' In short, I saw it was possible to realize the Rajah's whim. All that has been done, that can be done, will be done in machinery. I set to work, and in this iron-plated case, in the shape of an elephant, I managed to enclose the boiler, the machinery, and the tender of a traction-engine, with all its accessories. The flexible trunk, which can be raised and lowered at will, is the chimney; the legs of my animal are connected with the wheels of the apparatus; I arranged his eyes so as to dart out two jets of electric light, and the artificial elephant was complete. But as it was not my own spontaneous creation, I met with numerous difficulties which delayed me. The gigantic plaything, as you may call it, cost me many a sleepless night; so many indeed, that my rajah, who was wild with impatience, and passed the best part of his time in my workshops, died before the finishing touches were given that would allow the elephant to set forth on his travels. The poor fellow had no time even to make one trial of his invention. His heirs, however, less fanciful than he, viewed the apparatus with the terror of superstition, and as the work of a madman. They were only eager to get rid of it at any price. I therefore bought it up on the colonel's account. Now you know all the why and wherefore of the matter, and how it is that in all the world we alone are the proprietors of a steam elephant, with the strength of eighty horses, not to mention eighty elephants!"

"Bravo, Banks! well done!" exclaimed Captain Hood. "A first-class engineer who is an artist, a poet in iron and steel into the bargain, is a *rara avis* amongst us!"

"The rajah being dead," resumed Banks, "and his apparatus being in my possession, I had not the heart to destroy my elephant, and give the locomotive its ordinary form."

"And you did well!" replied the captain, "Our elephant is superb, there's no other word for it!" said the captain. "And what a fine effect we shall have, careering over the plains and through the jungles of Hindoostan! It is a regular rajah-like idea, isn't it? and one of which we shall reap the advantage, shan't we, colonel?"

Colonel Munro made a faint attempt at a smile, to show that he quite approved of the captain's speech.

The journey was resolved upon then and there; and now this unique and wonderful steam elephant was reduced to drag the travelling residence of four Englishmen, instead of stalking along in state with one of the most opulent rajahs of the Indian peninsula.

I quote the following description of the mechanism of this road engine, on which Banks had brought to bear all the improvements of modern science, from notes made at the time.

"Between the four wheels are all the machinery of cylinders, pistons, feed-pump, &c., covered by the body of the boiler. This tubular boiler is in the fore part of the elephant's body, and the tender, carrying fuel and water, in the hinder part. The boiler and tender, though both on the same truck, have a space between them, left for the use of the stoker. The engine-driver is stationed in the fire-proof howdah on the animal's back, in which we all could take refuge in case of any serious attack. He has there everything in his power, safety-valves, regulating brakes, &c., so that he can steer or back his engine at will. He has also thick lens-shaped glass fixed in the narrow embrasures, through which he can see the road both before and behind him.

"The boiler and tender are fixed on springs of the best

steel, so as to lessen the jolting caused by the inequalities of the ground. The wheels, constructed with vast solidity, are grooved so as to bite the earth, and prevent them from 'skating.'

"The nominal strength of the engine is equal to that of eighty horses, but its power can be increased to equal that of 150, without any danger of an explosion. A case, hermetically sealed, encloses all the machinery, so as to protect it from the dust of the roads, which would soon put the mechanism out of order. The machine has a double cylinder after the Field system, and its great perfection consists in this, that the expenditure is small and the results great. Nothing could be better arranged in that way, for in the furnace any kind of fuel may be burnt, either wood or coal. The engineer estimates the ordinary speed at fifteen miles an hour, but on a good road it can reach twenty-five. There is no danger of the wheels skating, not only from the grooves, but because of the perfect poise of the apparatus, which is all so well balanced that not even the severest jolting could disturb it. The atmospheric brakes, with which the engine is provided, could in a moment produce either a slackening of speed or a sudden halt.

"The facility with which the machine can ascend slopes is remarkable. Banks has succeeded most happily in this, taking into consideration the weight and power of propul-

THE IRON GIANT.

sion of the machine. It can easily ascend a slope at an inclination of from four to five inches in the yard, which is considerable."

There is a perfect network of magnificent roads made by the English all over India, which are excellently fitted for this mode of locomotion. The Great Trunk Road, for instance, stretches uninterruptedly for 1200 miles.

I must now describe the Steam House.

Banks had not only bought from the Nabob's heirs the traction-engine, but the train which it had in tow. This had of course been constructed, according to the oriental taste of the rajah, in the most gorgeous Hindoo fashion. I have already called it a travelling bungalow, and it merited the name, for the two cars composing it were simply a marvellous specimen of the architecture of the country.

Imagine two pagoda-shaped buildings without minarets, but with double-ridged roofs surmounted by a dome, the corbelling of the windows supported by sculptured pilasters, all the ornamentation in exquisitely carved and coloured woods of rare kinds, a handsome verandah both back and front. You might suppose them a couple of pagodas torn from the sacred hill of Sonnaghur.

To complete the marvel of this prodigious locomotive, I must add that it can float! In fact, the stomach, or that part of the elephant's body which contains the machinery, as well as the lower portion of the buildings, form boats of light steel. When a river is met with, the elephant marches straight into it, the train follows, and as the animal's feet can be moved by paddle-wheels, the Steam House moves gaily over the surface of the water. This is an indescribable advantage for such a vast country as India, where there are more rivers than bridges.

This was the train ordered by the capricious Rajah of Bhootan. But though the carriages were like pagodas on the outside, Banks thought it best to furnish the interior, to suit English tastes, with everything necessary for a long journey, and in this he was very successful.

The width of the two carriages was not less than eighteen feet; they therefore projected over the wheels, as the axles were not more than fifteen. Being well hung on splendid springs, any jolting would be as little felt as on a well made railroad.

The first carriage was forty-five feet long. In front, was an elegant verandah, in which a dozen people could sit comfortably. Two windows and a door led into the drawing-room, lighted besides by two side windows. This room, furnished with a table and book-case, and having luxurious divans all round it, was artistically decorated and hung with rich tapestry. A thick Turkey carpet covered the floor. "Tatties," or blinds, hung before the windows, and were kept moistened with perfumed water, so that a delightful freshness was constantly diffused throughout all the apartments. A punkah was suspended from the ceiling and kept continually in motion, for it was necessary to provide against the heat, which at certain times of the year is something frightful.

Opposite the verandah door was another of valuable wood, opening into the dining-room, which was lighted not only by side windows but by a ceiling of ground glass. Eight guests might have been comfortably seated round the table in the centre, so as we were but four we had ample room. It was furnished with sideboards and buffets loaded with all the wealth of silver, glass, and china, which is necessary to English comfort. Of course all these fragile articles were put in specially made racks, as is done on board ship, so that even on the roughest roads they would be perfectly safe.

A door led out into the passage, which ended in another verandah at the back. From this passage opened four rooms, each containing a bed, dressing-table, wardrobe and sofa, and fitted up like the cabins of the best transatlantic steamers. The first of these rooms on the left was occupied by Colonel Munro, the second on the right by Banks. Captain Hood was established next to the engineer, and I next to Sir Edward.

The second carriage was thirty-six feet in length, and also possessed a verandah which opened into a large kitchen, flanked on each side with a pantry, and supplied with everything that could be wanted. This kitchen communicated with a passage which, widening into a square in the middle, and lighted by a skylight, formed a dining-room for the servants. In the four angles were four cabins, occupied by Sergeant McNeil, the engine-driver, the stoker, and Colonel Munro's orderly; while at the back were two other rooms for the cook and Captain Hood's man; besides a gun-room, box-room, and ice-house, all opening into the back verandah.

It could not be denied that Banks had intelligently and comfortably arranged and furnished Steam House. There was an apparatus for heating it in winter with hot air from the engine, besides two small fireplaces in the drawing and dining-rooms. We were therefore quite prepared to brave the rigours of the cold season, even on the slopes of the mountains of Thibet.

You may be sure the important question of provisions had not been neglected, and we carried sufficient to feed the entire expedition for a year. They consisted chiefly of tins of preserved meat of the best brands, principally boiled and stewed beef, and also "mourghis," or fowls, of which there is so large a consumption all over India.

Thanks to the new inventions which allow both milk and soup to be carried in a concentrated form, we had abundance of both, the former for breakfast and the latter for tiffin, or luncheon.

After being exposed to evaporation, in a manner to render it of a pasty consistency, the milk is enclosed in hermetically-sealed tins, each of which, on the addition of water, supplies three quarts of good and nourishing milk. The soup, too, is condensed in much the same way, and is carried in tablets.

As I said, we had an ice-house, in which that luxury, so useful in hot climates, could be easily produced by means of the Carré apparatus, which causes a lowering of the temperature by means of the evaporation of liquid ammoniac gas. Either in this way or by the volatilization of methylated ether, the product of our sport could be indefinately preserved by the application of a process invented by a Frenchman, a compatriot of my own, Ch. Tellier. This was a valuable resource, as at all times it placed at our disposal food of the first quality. The cellar was well supplied as to beverages. French wines, different kinds of beer, brandy, arrack, occupied special places, and in quantities to satisfy the ideas of the most thirsty souls.

Our journey would lead us through many inhabited provinces. India is by no means a desert, and if one does not spare rupees, it is ease to procure, not only the necessaries, but also the superfluities of life. Perhaps if we were to winter in the northern regions, at the base of the Himalayas, we might be compelled to fall back on our own resources, but in any case it was not difficult to provide for all the exigencies of a comfortable existence. The practical mind of our friend Banks had foreseen everything, and we trusted to him to revictual us *en route*.

The following is the itinerary of the journey which was agreed on, subject to any modifications which unforeseen circumstances might suggest. We proposed leaving Calcutta, to follow the valley of the Ganges up to Allahabad, to cross the kingdom of Oude, so as to reach the first slopes of Thibet, to remain there for some months, sometimes in one place, sometimes in another, so as to give Captain Hood plenty of opportunity for hunting, and then to redescend to Bombay. We had thus 900 leagues, or 2700 miles before us. But our house and servants travelled with us. Under these conditions, who would refuse even to make the tour of the world again and again?

CHAPTER VI.

FIRST STAGES.

BEFORE dawn, on the morning of our start, I left the Spencer Hotel one of the best in Calcutta, which I had made my residence ever since my arrival.

The great city was by this time quite familiar to me. Morning promenades before the heat became unbearable; evening drives on the Strand, as far as the Esplanade or Fort William, where the splendid equipages of the English whirl scornfully past the not less splendid carriages of the great fat native baboos; expeditions through the curious streets of shops, which are very appropriately called bazaars; visits to the burial-grounds on the banks of the Ganges; to the Botanic Gardens, the work of the great naturalist Hooker; and to "Madam Kâli" the horrible four-armed woman, who, as the fierce goddess of death, is enshrined in a small temple where modern civilization and native barbarism are exhibited side by side. All this I had done. I had gazed at the vice-regal palace opposite the Spencer Hotel; admired the curious buildings on the Chowringhi Road, and the Town Hall, dedicated to the memory of the great men of our time; studied in detail the interesting mosque of Hougly; gone over the harbour crowded by the finest vessels of the English merchant service; made the acquaintance of the "adjutants," those singular birds known by a variety of names, whose vocation it is to act as scavengers and preserve the city in a perfectly salubrious condition. And all this being accomplished, I had now nothing to do but to take my departure. Accordingly, on the 6th of May, a wretched vehicle with two horses and four wheels, called a "palkighari," a machine unfit to be seen beside comfortable English-built carriages, came to convey me to the door of Colonel Munro's bungalow.

Our train awaited us at no great distance; we had only to enter and establish ourselves. Our luggage had of course been put "on board." Nothing unnecessary was allowed; but Captain Hood had large ideas in the matter of fire-arms, and considered an arsenal of four Enfield rifles, four fowling-pieces, two duck-guns, and several other guns, pistols and revolvers, quite indispensable for such a party as ours. This armoury appeared to threaten the lives of wild beasts rather than simply to supply game for our table, but the Nimrod of our expedition was very decided in his views on the subject.

FIRST STAGES. 83

Captain Hood was in the highest spirits.

The triumph of having succeeded in persuading Colonel Munro to forsake his solitary retreat; the pleasure of setting out on such a tour, with an equipage so entirely novel; the prospect of unusual occupation, plenty of exercise, and grand Himalayan excursions; all combined to excite him to the greatest degree; and he gave vent to his feelings in perpetual exclamations, while he urged us to bestir ourselves.

The clock struck the hour of departure. Steam was up, the engine ready for action. Our engine-driver stood at his post, his hand on the regulator. The whistle sounded.

"Off with you, Behemoth!" shouted Captain Hood, waving his cap.

And this name, so well suited to our wonderful traction-engine, was ever after bestowed upon it.

Now for a word as to our attendants, who occupied the second house—No. 2, as we used to call it.

The engine-driver, Storr, was an Englishman, and had been employed on "The Great Southern" line until a few months previously. Banks knew him to be an efficient and clever workman, thoroughly up to his business, and therefore engaged him for Colonel Munro's service. He was a man of forty years of age, and proved exceedingly useful to us.

The fireman's name was Kâlouth. He belonged to a tribe or class of Hindoos much sought after by railway companies, to be employed as stokers, because they endure with impunity the double heat of their tropical climate and that of the engine furnaces. They resemble, in this, the Arabs employed as firemen in the Red Sea steamers—good fellows who are content to be merely boiled where Europeans would be roasted in a few minutes.

Colonel Munro had a regimental servant named Goûmi, one of the tribe of Gourkas. He belonged to that regiment which, as an act of good discipline, had accepted the use of the Enfield rifles, the introduction of which into the service had been the reason, or at least the pretext, of the sepoy revolt. Small, active, supple, and of tried fidelity, Goûmi always wore the dark uniform of the rifle brigade, which was as dear to him as his own skin.

Sergeant McNeil and Goûmi were attached heart and soul to Colonel Munro.

They had fought under his command all through the Indian campaign; they had accompanied him in his fruitless search for Nana Sahib; they had followed him into retirement, and would never dream of leaving him.

But Captain Hood had also a faithful follower—a frank, lively young Englishman, whose name was Fox, and who would not have changed places with any officer's servant under the sun. He perfectly adored Captain Hood, and was quite as keen a sportsman as his master.

Having accompanied him on numberless tiger-hunts. Fox had proved his skill, and reckoned the tigers which had fallen to his gun at thirty-seven, only three less than his master could boast of.

Our staff of attendants was completed by a negro cook, whose dominion lay in the forepart of the second house. He was of French origin, and having boiled, fried, and fricaseed in every possible latitude, Monsieur Parazard—for that was his name—had no small opinion of the importance of his noble profession; he would have scorned to call it his trade.

He presided over his saucepans with the air of a high priest, and distributed his condiments with the accuracy of a chemist. Monsieur Parazard was vain, it is true, but so clever that we readily pardoned his vanity.

Our expedition, then, was made up of ten persons; namely, Sir Edward Munro, Banks, Hood, and myself, who were accommodated in one house; McNeil, Storr, Kâlouth, Goûmi, Fox, and Monsieur Parazard, in the other.

I must not forget the two dogs, Fan and Niger, whose sporting qualities were to be put to the proof by Hood, in many a stirring episode of the chase.

Bengal is perhaps, if not the most curious, at least the

richest of the three Indian presidencies. It is now, properly speaking, the country of the Rajahs, which lies more especially in the centre of the vast empire, but the province extends over a district the dense population of which may be considered essentially Hindoo.

The route we proposed to take would lead us obliquely across this district, which to the extreme north is bounded by the insurmountable barriers of the Himalaya chain.

After some discussion, it was finally proposed that, having travelled up the banks of the Hoogly for some leagues (the Hoogly being that branch of the river Ganges which passes through Calcutta), we should leave to the right the French town of Chandernagore, thence follow the line of the railroad as far as Burdwan, and afterwards pass transversely through Behar, so as to rejoin the Ganges at Benares.

"Arrange the route exactly as you please, my friends," said Colonel Munro. "Decide without reference to me. Whatever you do will be done well."

"Still, my dear Munro," replied Banks, "it would be satisfactory to have your opinion."

"No, Banks," returned the colonel; "I give myself up to you, and have no wish to visit one place rather than another. One single question, however, I will ask. After Benares, in what direction do you propose to travel?"

"Northwards, most certainly," exclaimed Hood impetuously. "Right across the kingdom of Oude, up to the lower ranges of the Himalayas!"

"Well then, my friends," began Colonel Munro, "perhaps when we get so far, I will propose—but it will be soon enough to speak of that when the time comes. Till then, go just where you choose."

I could not help feeling somewhat surprised by these words of Sir Edward Munro. What could he have in his mind? Had he only agreed to take this journey in the hope that chance might serve his purpose better than his own will and endeavour had done? Did it seem to him possible that, supposing Nana Sahib to be still alive, he might yet find trace of him in the extreme north of India? Was the hope of vengeance still strong within him?

I could not resist the conviction that our friend was influenced by this hidden motive, and that Sergeant McNeil shared his master's thoughts.

When we left Calcutta we were seated in the drawing-room of Steam House. The door and the windows of the verandah were open, and the measured beat of the punkah kept up an agreeable temperature.

Storr drove the engine at a slow and steady rate of three miles an hour, for we travellers were just then in no haste, and desired to see at leisure the country we passed through.

For a long time we were followed by a number of Europeans who were astonished at our equipage, and by crowds of natives whose wonder and admiration was mingled with fear. We gradually distanced this attendant mob, but met people continually who lavished upon us admiring exclamations of "Wallah! wallah!" The huge elephant, vomiting clouds of steam, excited far more astonishment than the two superb cars which he drew after him.

At ten o'clock breakfast was served in the dining-room; and, seated at a table which was far less shaken than it would have been in a first-class railway carriage, we did ample justice to the culinary skill of Monsieur Parazard.

We were travelling along the left bank of the Hoogly, the most western of the numerous arms of the Ganges, which form together the labyrinthine network of the delta of the Sunderbunds, and is entirely an alluvial formation.

"What you see there, my dear Maucler," said Banks, "is a conquest won by the sacred river Ganges from the not less sacred Bay of Bengal. It has been a mere affair of time. There is probably not an atom of that soil which has not been transported hither, by the mighty current, from the Himalayan heights. Little by little the stream has robbed the mountains in order to form this province, through which it has worked its bed—"

"And changes incessantly!" broke in Captain Hood. "There never was such a whimsical capricious lunatic of a river as this same Ganges. People take the trouble to build a town on its banks, and behold, a few centuries later the town is in the midst of a plain, its harbours are dry, the river has changed its course! Thus Rajmahal, as well as Gaur, were both formerly situated on this faithless stream, and now there they are dying of thirst amidst the parched rice-fields of the plains."

"Then may not some such fate be in store for Calcutta?" inquired I.

"Ah, who knows."

"Come, come," said Banks; "you forget the engineers! It would only require skilful embankments. We could easily put a straight waistcoat on the Ganges, and restrain its vagaries."

"It is well for you, Banks," said I, "that no natives are within earshot when you speak so irreverently of their sacred stream! They would never forgive you."

"Well, really," returned Banks, "they look on their river as a son of God, if not God himself, and in their eyes it can do nothing amiss."

"Not even by maintaining, as it does, epidemics of the plague, fever, and cholera!" cried Captain Hood. "I must say, however, that the atmosphere it engenders agrees splendidly with the tigers and crocodiles which swarm in the

Sunderbunds. Ah, the savages! Fox!" he added, turning to his servant, who was clearing away the breakfast-things.

"Yes, captain."

"Wasn't it there you killed your thirty-seventh?"

"Yes, captain, two miles from Fort Canning. It was one evening—"

"There, Fox! that will do," interrupted the captain, as he tossed off a large glass of brandy and soda. "I know all about the thirty-seventh. The history of your thirty-eighth would interest me more."

"My thirty-eighth is not killed yet, captain."

"No, but you will bag him some day, Fox, as I shall my forty-first."

It is to be noted, that in the conversations of Captain Hood and his man, the word "tiger" was never mentioned. It was quite unnecessary. The two hunters perfectly understood one another.

As we proceeded to the Hoogly, its banks, which above Calcutta are rather low, gradually contracted, much reducing the width of the river.

This part of the country is subject to formidable cyclones, which spread disaster far and wide.

Whole districts wasted, hundreds of houses heaped one upon another, immense plantations devastated, thousands of corpses strewing the soil; such is the ruin left behind when these fearful atmospheric disturbances sweep over the land, and of which the cyclone of 1864 was a most terrible example.

It is well known that the climate of India is varied by three seasons: the rainy season, the cold season, and the hot season. The last is the shortest, but also the most trying. March, April, and May, are months particularly to be dreaded. May is, of all these, the hottest, and those Europeans who then venture to face the noontide blaze of the sun, do it at the risk of their lives.

It is not unusual for the thermometer to rise in the shade to 106 degrees Fahrenheit.

"Men are forced," writes M. de Valbezen," to wheeze in breathing, like broken-winded horses, and during the war both officers and soldiers were frequently obliged to dash water over their heads to prevent congestion of the brain."

We did not, however, suffer from the heat, as besides the draught produced by the motion of our Steam House, the punkahs kept fanning into pleasant circulation the humid air which blew through the woven grass blinds stretched across our windows, and which were constantly watered.

The rainy season, which lasts from June till October, was not far distant, and in some respects might prove more disagreeable than the hot months. But, luxuriously provided as we were, we had little to fear under any conditions of the atmosphere. About one o'clock in the afternoon, having enjoyed a most agreeable drive at a gentle pace, we arrived at Chandernagore.

I had already visited this little corner of territory—all that remains to France in the whole presidency of Bengal. Chandernagore, the ancient rival of Calcutta during the struggles of the eighteenth century, remains under the protection of the tri-coloured flag, but has no right to maintain a garrison of more than fifteen men. The town is now fallen into decay; it is without trade, industry, or commerce; its bazaars are deserted; its forts abandoned. If the Allahabad railroad had at least passed outside its walls, Chandernagore might have recovered some vitality; but, anticipating the demands of the French Government, the English railway company took pains to distort the line, so as to skirt our territory, and Chandernagore has thus lost her only chance of retrieving her fortunes and resuming some measure of commercial importance.

We did not enter the town, but halted three miles off, on the borders of a grove of palm-trees.

When our camp was pitched one would have taken it for a rising young village; but being movable, it proceeded on its way early next morning, after a peaceful night, during which we all slept soundly in our comfortable bed-rooms.

FIRST STAGES.

During the halt, Banks had attended to the supply of fuel. The engine did not consume much; but it was necessary to have on the tender sufficient water, wood, and coal to keep us going for sixty hours.

This rule about keeping up the supply was carefully applied by Captain Hood and his faithful Fox to the maintenance of their own particular furnaces; that is to say, their stomachs, which, in truth, were always amply provided with the sort of fuel so necessary to keep up the powers of the human machine.

The next stage was to be longer. By travelling for two days, stopping only during the night, we could reach Burdwan, and visit that city on the 9th of May.

At six o'clock in the morning Storr sounded his shrill whistle, and the iron giant started at a more rapid rate than that of the preceding day.

For some hours we kept near the railroad, which from Burdwan passes on to Rajmahal, in the valley of the Ganges, which it then follows till beyond Benares.

The Calcutta train passed us at great speed, and the shouts of the passengers showed that while they admired us, they mocked our slower pace. We did not return their defiance. More rapidly they certainly did travel than ourselves, but in comfort there was simply no comparison.

During these two days the scenery was invariably flat, and therefore monotonous. Here and there waved a few slender cocoanut-trees, the last of which we should leave behind after passing Burdwan. These trees, which belong to the great family of palms, are partial to the coast, and love to breathe salt air. Thus they are not found beyond a somewhat narrow belt along the sea coast, and it is vain to seek them in Central India. The flora of the interior is, however, extremely interesting and varied.

On each side of our route, the country in this part resembles an immense chess-board marked out in squares of rice-fields, and stretching as far as we could see. Shades of green predominated, and the harvest promised to be abundant in this moist warm soil, the prodigious fertility of which is well known.

On the evening of the second day, with punctuality which an express might have envied, the engine gave its last snort and stopped at the gates of Burdwan. This city is the judicial headquarters of an English district; but properly speaking, the country belongs to a Maharajah, who pays taxes to Government amounting to not less than ten millions.

The town consists in a great part, of low houses, standing in fine avenues of trees, such as cocoanuts and arequipas. These avenues being wide enough to admit our train, we proceeded to encamp in a charming spot, full of shade and freshness.

It seemed as though a large addition were suddenly

made to the city, when our houses took up their position in it, and we would not have exchanged our residences for any in the splendid quarter where stands the magnificent palace of the sovereign of Burdwan.

It may well be supposed that our elephant produced all the terror and admiration which he usually excited among Bengalees. The people ran together from all sides, the men bare-headed, their hair cut short *à la* Titus, and wearing only loose cotton drawers, while the women were enveloped from head to foot in white.

"I begin to be afraid," said Captain Hood, "that the Maharajah will want to buy our Behemoth, and that he will offer such a vast sum, we shall be forced to let his highness have him."

"Never!" exclaimed Banks. "I will make another elephant for him if he likes, of power enough to draw his whole capital from one end of his dominion to the other. But we won't part with Behemoth at any price, will we, Munro?"

"Most certainly we will not," answered the colonel, in the tone of a man who was not to be tempted by millions.

And after all there was no question as to whether our colossal elephant was for sale or not. The Maharajah was not at Burdwan, and the only visit we received was from his "kamdar," a sort of private secretary, who came to examine our equipage. Having done so, this personage offered us permission, which we very readily accepted, to examine the gardens of the palace.

We found them well worth a visit. They were beautifully laid out, filled with the finest specimens of tropical vegetation, and watered by sparkling rivulets flowing from miniature lakes. The park we also admired greatly: its verdant lawns were adorned by fanciful kiosks, and in superb menageries we found specimens of all the animals of the country, wild as well as domestic. Here were goats, stags, deer, elephants, tigers, lions, panthers, and bears, besides others too numerous to mention.

"Oh, captain!" cried Fox, "here are tigers in cages just like birds. Isn't it a pity?"

"Indeed, Fox, and so it is," replied the captain. "If the poor fellows had their choice, they certainly would far rather be prowling about in the jungle, even within *reach of our rifle-balls!*"

"That's just what I think, captain," sighed honest Fox.

Next morning, the 10th of May, having laid in a fresh stock of provisions, we quitted Burdwan. Our Steam House passed the line of railroad by a level crossing, and travelled in the direction of Ramghur, a town situated about seventy leagues from Calcutta.

It is true that by pursuing this route we left several places unvisited: as, for instance, the important town of

Moorshedabad, which is not interesting, either in its native or European aspect; Monghir, a sort of Hindoo Birmingham, perched on a high promontory overhanging the course of the sacred river; and Patna, the capital of the kingdom of Behar, through which we intended to pass obliquely. This city seems almost smothered in the creeping plants which so abound in its neighbourhood as to invade its walls and houses on all sides. It is the wealthy centre of the opium trade. But we had a greater object in view, and therefore followed a more southern route, about two degrees below the valley of the Ganges.

During this part of the journey Behemoth was kept going at a gentle trot, which pace proved the excellent structure of our well-hung carriages; the roads being good also favoured our experiment.

To the great surprise of Captain Hood, we passed through many jungles without seeing any wild animals. It seemed not unlikely that they were terrified, and fled at the approach of a gigantic elephant, vomiting steam and smoke; but as it was to the northern regions, and not to Bengal provinces, that our hunter looked for the sport he loved so well, he did not as yet begin to complain.

On the 15th of May we were near Ramghur, about fifty leagues from Burdwan. The rate of speed at which we had travelled was not more than fifteen leagues in twelve hours.

Three days afterwards, on the 18th, we stopped at the little town of Chittra.

No incidents marked these stages of our journey. The heat was intense; but what could be more agreeable than a siesta beneath the cool shelter of the verandahs! The burning hours passed away in luxurious repose.

In the evenings Storr and Kâlouth cleaned the furnace and oiled and thoroughly examined the engine, operations which were always carefully superintended by Banks himself. While he was so employed, Captain Hood and I accompanied by Fox, Goûmi, and the two dogs, used to take our guns, and explore the neighbourhood of our camp. We fell in with nothing more important in the way of game than birds and a few small animals; and although the captain turned up his nose at such poor sport, he was always highly delighted next day, when Monsieur Parazard regaled us with a variety of new and savoury dishes.

Banks, when he could, made our halting-places near some wood, and on the banks of a stream or brook, because it was always necessary to replenish the tender with what was wanted for the next day's journey, and he attended personally to every detail.

Goûmi and Fox were frequently employed as hewers of wood and drawers of water.

When the day's work was done we lighted our cigars (excellent Manilla cheroots), and while we smoked we talked about this country with which Hood, as well as Banks, was so thoroughly well acquainted. The captain disdained cigars, and his vigorous lungs inhaled, through a pipe twenty feet long, the aromatic smoke of a "hookah," carefully filled for him by the hand of Fox. It was our greatest wish that Colonel Munro should accompany us on our little shooting excursions round the camp. We invariably asked him to do so, but he as invariably declined, and remained with Sergeant McNeil, spending the time of our absence in pacing up and down a distance of not more than a hundred yards.

They spoke little, but so completely did they understand one another, that words were not needed for the interchange of thoughts.

Both were absorbed in tragic and indelible recollections. It was possible that, in approaching the theatre of the bloody insurrection, these recollections would become more vivid.

Banks and Captain Hood shared with me the opinion that some fixed idea, which would be developed later, had induced Colonel Munro to join us in this expedition to the north of India.

In that case we might be on the verge of great events. Our steam Behemoth might be drawing us across these huge plains and mountains to the scene of a thrilling and unexpected drama.

CHAPTER VII.

THE PILGRIMS OF THE PHALGOU RIVER.

WHAT is now called Behar was in former days the empire of Magadha. In the time of the Buddhists it was sacred territory, and is still covered with temples and monasteries. But, for many centuries, the Brahmins have occupied the place of the priests of Buddha. They have taken possession of the "viharas" or temples, and, turning them to their own account, live on the produce of the worship they teach. The faithful flock thither from all parts, and in these sacred places the Brahmins compete with the holy waters of the Ganges, the pilgrimages to Benares, the ceremonies of Juggernaut; in fact, one may say the country belongs to them.

The soil is rich, there are immense rice-fields of emerald green, and vast plantations of poppies. There are numerous villages, buried in luxuriant verdure, and shaded by palms, mangoes and date-trees, over which nature has thrown, like a net, a tangled web of creeping plants.

Steam House passed along roads which were embowered in foliage, and beneath the leafy arches the air was cool and fresh. We followed the chart of our route, and had no fear of losing our way.

The snorting and trumpeting of our elephant, mingled with the deafening screams of the winged tribes and the discordant chatterings and scoldings of apes and monkeys, and the golden fruit of the bananas, shone like stars through light clouds, as smoke and steam rolled in volumes among the trees. The delicate rice-birds rose in flocks as Behemoth passed along, their white plumage almost concealed as they flew through the spiral wreaths of steam.

Here and there the thick woods opened out into detached groups of banyans, groves of shaddocks, and beds of "dahl" (a sort of arborescent pea, which grows on stalks about a yard high), and glimpses were then obtained of landscapes in the background.

But the heat! the moist air scarcely made its way through the tatties of our windows. The hot winds, charged with caloric as they passed over the surface of the great western plains, enveloped the land in their fiery embrace.

One longs for the month of June, when this state of the atmosphere will be modified. Death threatens those who seek to brave the stroke of this flaming sun.

The fields are deserted. Even the "ryots" themselves,

inured as they are to the burning heat, cannot continue their agricultural labours. The shady roadway alone is practicable, and even there we require the shelter of our travelling bungalow. Kâlouth the fireman must be made of pure carbon, or he would certainly dissolve before the grating of his furnace. But the brave Hindoo holds out nobly. It has become second nature with him, this existence on the platform of the locomotives which scour the railway lines of Central India!

During the daytime of May the 19th, the thermometer suspended on the wall of the dining-room registered 106 degrees Fahrenheit. That evening we were unable to take our accustomed "constitutional" or "hawakana." This word signifies literally "to eat air," and means that, after the stifling heat of the tropical day, people go out to inhale the cool pure air of evening. On this occasion we felt that, on the contrary, the air would eat us!

"Monsieur Maucler," said Sergeant McNeil to me, "this heat reminds me of one day in March, when Sir Hugh Rose, with just two pieces of artillery, tried to storm the walls at Lucknow. It was sixteen days since we had crossed the river Betwa, and during all that time our horses had not once been unsaddled. We were fighting between enormous walls of granite, and we might as well have been in a burning fiery furnace. The "chitsis" passed up and down our ranks, carrying water in their leathern bottles, which they poured on the mens' heads as they stood to their guns, otherwise we should have dropped. Well do I remember how I felt! I was exhausted, my skull was ready to burst—I tottered. Colonel Munro saw me, and snatching the bottle from the hand of a chitsi, he emptied it over me—and it was the last water the carriers could procure. . . . A man can't forget that sort of thing, sir! No, no! When I have shed the last drop of my blood for my colonel, I shall still be in his debt."

"Sergeant McNeil," said I, "does it not seem to you that since we left Calcutta, Colonel Munro has become more absent and melancholy than ever? I think that every day—"

"Yes, sir," replied McNeil, hastily interrupting me, "but that is quite natural. My colonel is approaching Lucknow—Cawnpore—where Nana Sahib murdered. . . . Ah, it drives me mad to speak of it! Perhaps it would have been better if this journey had been planned in some different direction—if we had avoided the provinces ravaged by the insurrection! The recollection of these awful events is not yet softened by time."

"Why not even now change the route?" exclaimed I. "If you like, McNeil, I will speak about it to Mr. Banks and Captain Hood."

"It's too late now," replied the sergeant. "Besides, I have reason to think that my colonel wishes to revisit, perhaps for the last time, the theatre of that horrible war; that he will once more go to the scene of Lady Munro's death."

"If you really think so, McNeil," said I, "it will be better to let things take their course, and not attempt to alter our plans. It is often felt to be a consolation to weep at the grave of those who are dear to us."

"Yes, at their grave!" cried McNeil. "But who can call the well of Cawnpore a grave? Could that fearful spot seem to anybody like a quiet grave in a Scotch churchyard, where, among flowers and under shady trees, they would stand on a spot, marked by a stone with one name, just one, upon it? Ah, sir, I fear the colonel's grief will be something terrible! But I tell you again, it is too late to change the route. If we did, who knows but he might refuse to follow it? No, no; let things be, and may God direct us!"

It was evident, from the way in which McNeil spoke, that he well knew what was certain to influence his master's plans, and I was by no means convinced that the opportunity of revisiting Cawnpore had not led the colonel to quit Calcutta. At all events, he now seemed attracted as by a magnet to the scene where that fatal tragedy had been enacted. To that force it would be necessary to yield.

I proceeded to ask the sergeant whether he himself had

relinquished the idea of revenge—in other words, whether he believed Nana Sahib to be dead.

"No," replied McNeil frankly. "Although I have no ground whatever for my belief, I feel persuaded that Nana Sahib will not die unpunished for his many crimes. No; I have heard nothing, I know nothing about him, but I am inwardly convinced it is so. Ah, sir! righteous vengeance is something to live for! Heaven grant that my presentiment is true, and then—some day—"

The sergeant left his sentence unfinished, but his looks were sufficient. The servant and the master were of one mind.

When I reported this conversation to Banks and the captain, they were both of opinion that no change of route ought to be made. It had never been proposed to go to Cawnpore; and, once across the Ganges at Benares, we intended to push directly northwards, traversing the eastern portion of the kingdoms of Oude and Rohilkund. McNeil might after all be wrong in supposing that Sir Edward Munro would wish to revisit Cawnpore; but if he proposed to do so, we determined to offer no opposition.

As to Nana Sahib, if there had been any truth in the report of his reappearance in the Bombay presidency, we ought by this time to have heard something more of him. But, on the contrary, all the intelligence we could gain on our route led to the conclusion that the authorities had been in error.

If Colonel Munro really had any ulterior design in making this journey, it might have seemed more natural that he should have confided his intentions to Banks, who was his most intimate friend, rather than to Sergeant McNeil. But the latter was no doubt preferred, because he would urge his master to undertake what Banks would probably consider perilous and imprudent enterprises.

At noon, on the 19th of May, we left the small town of Chittra, 280 miles from Calcutta.

Next day, at nightfall, we arrived, after a day of fearful heat, in the neighbourhood of Gaya.

The halt was made on the banks of a sacred river, the Phalgou, well known to pilgrims.

Our two houses were drawn up on a pretty bank, shaded by fine trees, within a couple of miles of the town. This place, being, as I mentioned before, extremely curious and interesting, we intended to remain in it for thirty-six hours, that is to say for two nights and a day. Starting about four o'clock next morning, in order to avoid the mid-day heat, Banks, Captain Hood, and I, left Colonel Munro, and took our way to the town of Gaya.

It is stated that 150,000 devotees annually visit this centre of Brahminical institutions; and we found every road to the place was swarming with men, women, old people, and children, who were advancing from all directions across the country, having braved the thousand fatigues of a long pilgrimage in order to fulfil their religious duties.

We could not have had a better guide than Banks, who knew the neighbourhood well, having previously been on a survey in Behar, where a railroad was proposed, but not yet constructed.

Captain Hood, who never liked to miss the chance of a shot, would have carried his gun; but Banks, lest our Nimrod should be tempted to wander away from us induced him to leave it in camp.

Just before entering the place, which is appropriately called the Holy City, Banks stopped us near a sacred tree, round which pilgrims of every age and sex were bowed in the attitude of adoration.

This tree was a peepul: the girth of the trunk was enormous; but although many of its branches were decayed and fallen, it was not more than two or three hundred years old. This fact was ascertained by M. Louis Rousselet, two years later, during his interesting journey across the India of the Rajahs.

The "Tree of Buddha," as it is called, is the last of a generation of sacred peepuls, which have for ages overshadowed the spot, the first having been planted there five centuries before the Christian era; and probably the fanatics kneeling before it believe this to be the original tree consecrated there by Buddha. It stands upon a ruined terrace close to a temple built of brick, and evidently of great antiquity.

The appearance of three Europeans, in the midst of these swarming thousands of natives, was not regarded favourably. Nothing was said, but we could not reach the terrace, nor penetrate within the old temple: certainly it would have been difficult to do so under any circumstances, on account of the dense masses of pilgrims by whom the way was blocked up.

"I wish we could fall in with a Brahmin," said Banks; "we might then inspect the temple, and feel we were doing the thing thoroughly."

"What!" cried I, "would a priest be less strict than his followers?"

"My dear Maucler," answered Banks, "the strictest rules will give way before the offer of a few rupees! The Brahmins must live."

"I don't see why they should," bluntly said Captain Hood, who never professed toleration towards the Hindoos, nor held in respect, as his countrymen generally do, their manners, customs, prejudices, and objects of veneration.

In his eyes India was nothing but a vast hunting-ground, and he felt a far deeper interest in the wild inhabitants of the jungles than in the native population either of town or country.

After remaining for some time at the foot of the sacred tree, Banks led us on towards the town of Gaya, the crowd of pilgrims increasing as we advanced. Very soon, through a vista of verdure, the picturesque edifices of Gaya appeared on the summit of a rock.

It is the temple of Vishnu which attracts travellers to this place. The construction is modern, as it was rebuilt by the Queen of Holcar only a few years ago. The great curiosity of this temple are the marks left by Vishnu when he condescended to visit earth on purpose to contend with the demon Maya. The struggle between a god and a fiend could not long remain doubtful.

Maya succumbed, and a block of stone, visible within the enclosure of Vishnu-Pad, bears witness, by the deep impress of his adversary's foot-prints, that the demon had to deal with a formidable foe.

I said the block of stone was "visible;" I ought to have said "visible to Hindoo natives only." No European is permitted to gaze upon these divine relics.

Perhaps a more robust faith than is to be found in Western minds may be necessary in order to distinguish these traces on the miraculous stone. Be that as it may, Bank's offer of money failed this time. No priest would accept what would have been the price of a sacrilege; I dare not venture to suppose that the sum offered was unequal to the extent of the Brahminical conscience.

Anyhow, we could not get into the temple dedicated to that gentle good-looking young man of azure-blue colour, attired and crowned like a king of ancient times, and celebrated for his ten incarnations, who represents the "Preserver," as opposed to Siva, the ferocious "Destroyer," and is acknowledged by the Vaichnavas (or worshippers of Vishnu) to be chief among the three hundred and thirty million deities of this pre-eminently polytheistic mythology.

But we had no reason to regret our excursion to the Sacred City, nor to the Vishnu-Pad. It would be utterly impossible to describe the confused mass of temples and the endless succession of courts which we traversed. Theseus himself, with Ariadne's thread in his hand, would have been lost in such a labyrinth, and after all we were refused admittance to the sanctuary! We finally descended the rocky eminence of Gaya.

Captain Hood was furious. He seemed disposed to deal summarily with the Brahmin who had turned us away.

Banks had to restrain him forcibly.

"Are you mad, Hood?" said he. "Don't you know that the Hindoos regard their priests, the Brahmins, not merely as a race of illustrious descent, but also as beings of altogether superior and supernatural origin?"

When we reached that part of the river Phalgou which

bathes the rock of Gaya, the prodigious assemblage of pilgrims lay before us in its full extent. There, in indescribable confusion, was a heaving, huddling, jostling crowd of men and women, old men and children, citizens and peasants, rich baboos and poor ryots, of every imaginable degree; "Vaichyas," merchants and husbandmen, "Kchatryas," haughty native warriors; "Sudras," wretched artisans of different sorts; "Pariahs," beneath and outside all caste, whose very eyes defile the objects they look upon; in a word all classes and every caste in India. The vigorous, high-spirited Rajpoot elbowing the weak Bengalee, the natives of the Punjaub face to face with those of Scinde. Some came in palanquins, others in carriages drawn by large humped oxen. Some lie beside their camels, whose snake-like heads are stretched out on the ground, while many travel on foot from all parts of India. Here tents are set up; there carts and waggons are unyoked, and numerous huts made of branches are prepared as temporary shelter for the crowd.

"What a mob!" exclaimed Captain Hood.

"The water of the Phalgou will not be fit to drink this evening," observed Banks.

"Why not?" inquired I.

"Because its waters are sacred, and this unsavoury crowd will go and bathe in them, as they do in the Ganges."

"Are we down stream?" cried Hood, pointing towards our encampment.

"No! don't be uneasy, captain!" answered Banks laughing; "we are up the river."

"That's all right! It would never do to water Behemoth at an impure fountain!"

We passed on through thousands of natives massed together in comparatively small space. The ear was struck by a discordant noise of chains and small bells. It was thus that mendicants appealed to public charity. Infinitely varied specimens of this vagrant brotherhood swarmed in all directions. Most of them displayed false wounds and deformities, but although the professed beggars only pretend to be sufferers, it is very different with the religious fanatics. In fact it would be difficult to carry enthusiasm further than they do.

Some of the fakirs, nearly naked, were covered with ashes; one had his arm fixed in a painful position by prolonged tension, another had kept his hand closed until it was pierced by the nails of his own fingers.

Some had measured the whole distance of their journey by the length of their bodies. For hundreds of miles they had continued incessantly to lie down, rise up, and lie down again, as though acting the part of a surveyor's chain.

Here some of the faithful, stupefied with "bang" (which

is liquid opium mixed with a decoction of hemp), were suspended on branches of trees, by iron hooks plunged into their shoulders. Hanging thus, they whirled round and round until the flesh gave way, and they fell into the waters of the Phalgou.

Others, in honour of Siva, had pierced their arms, legs, or tongues through and through with little darts, and made serpents lick the blood which flowed from the wounds.

Such a spectacle could not be otherwise than repugnant to a European eye. I was passing on in haste, when Banks suddenly stopped me, saying,—

"The hour of prayer!"

At the same instant a Brahmin appeared in the midst of the crowd. He raised his right hand, and pointed towards the rising sun, hitherto concealed behind the rocks of Gaya.

The first ray darted by the glorious luminary was the signal. The all but naked crowd entered the sacred waters. There were simple immersions, as in the early form of baptism, but these soon changed into water parties of which it was not easy to perceive the religious character. Perhaps the initiated, who recited "slocas" or texts, which for a given sum the priests dictated to them, thought no more of the cleansing of their bodies than their souls. The truth being that after having taken a little water in the hollow of the hand, and sprinkled it towards the four cardinal points, they merely threw up a few drops into their faces, like bathers who amuse themselves on the beach as they enter the shallow waves. I ought to add besides, that they never forgot to pull out at least one hair for every sin they had committed.

A good many deserved to come forth bald from the waters of the Phalgou!

So vehement were the watery gambols of the faithful, as they plunged hither and thither, that the alligators in terror fled to the opposite bank. There they remained in a row, staring with their dull sea-green eyes at the noisy crowd which had invaded their domain, and making the air resound with the snapping of their formidable jaws. The pilgrims paid no more attention to them than if they had been harmless lizards.

It was time to leave these singular devotees, who were getting ready to enter Kaïlas, which is the paradise of Brahm; so we went up the river and returned to our encampment.

Breakfast awaited us; and the rest of the day, which was excessively hot, passed without incident.

Towards the evening Captain Hood went out shooting, and brought in some game.

Meantime, as we were to start at daybreak, Storr, Kâlouth, and Goûmi, took in supplies of wood and water, and made all necessary preparations. By nine in the evening we had retired to our bedrooms. The night was likely to be very calm but dark, for thick clouds obscured the stars, and made the atmosphere so heavy, that the heat continued as great as before sunset.

I found it difficult to fall asleep in temperature so stifling; my window was open, but the hot air which entered, seemed to me very unfit for the use of human lungs.

Midnight came, and I had not enjoyed an instant's repose. I was firmly resolved to sleep for two or three hours before our departure; but I made a mistake in supposing I could command the visit of slumber. The more I exerted my will in the effort, the further slumber fled from me, utterly refusing to obey the summons.

It might have been one o'clock in the morning when I thought I heard a dull murmuring sound approach along the banks of the Phalgou.

My first idea was, that the atmosphere being charged with electricity, a storm of wind was rising in the west which would displace the strata of air, and perhaps make it more suitable for respiration.

I was mistaken; the branches of the trees above us remained motionless; not a leaf stirred.

I put my head out at my window and listened. I plainly heard the distant murmur, but nothing was to be seen. The surface of the river was calm and placid, and the sound proceeded neither from the air nor from the water. Although puzzled, I could perceive no cause for alarm, and returning to bed, fatigue overcame my wakefulness, and I became drowsy. At intervals I was conscious of the inexplicable murmuring noise, but finally fell fast asleep.

In about two hours, just as the first rays of dawn broke through the darkness, I awoke with a start.

Some one in the passage was calling the engineer.

"Mr. Banks!"

"What is wanted?"

"Will you come here, sir?"

It was Storr the fireman who spoke to Banks.

I rose immediately, and joined them in the front verandah. Colonel Munro was already there, and Captain Hood came soon after.

"What's the matter?" I heard Banks say.

"Just you look, sir," replied Storr.

It was light enough for us to see the river banks, and part of the road which stretched away before us; and to our great surprise these were encumbered by several hundred Hindoos, who were lying about in groups.

"Ah! those are some of the pilgrims we saw yesterday!" said Captain Hood.

"But what are they doing here?" said I.

"No doubt," replied the captain, "they are waiting for sunrise, that they may perform their ablutions."

"No such thing," said Banks; "why should they leave Gaya to do that? I suspect they have come here because—"

"Because Behemoth has produced his usual effect," interrupted Captain Hood. They heard that a huge great elephant—a colossus—bigger than the biggest they ever saw, was in the neighbourhood, and of course they came to admire him."

"If they keep to admiration, it will be all very well," returned the engineer, shaking his head.

"What do you fear, Banks?" asked Colonel Munro.

"Well, I am afraid these fanatics may get in the way, and impede our progress."

"Be prudent, whatever you do! One cannot act too cautiously in dealing with such devotees."

"Kâlouth!" cried Banks, calling the stoker, "are the fires ready?"

"Yes, sir."

"Well, light up."

"Yes, light up by all means, Kâlouth," cried Captain Hood; "blaze away, Kâlouth; and let Behemoth puff smoke and steam into the ugly faces of all this rabble!"

It was then half-past three in the morning.

It would take half-an-hour to get up steam. The fires

were instantly lighted. The wood crackled in the furnaces and dense smoke issued from the gigantic trunk of the elephant, which was uplifted high among the boughs of the great trees.

Several parties of natives approached; then a general movement took place in the crowd. The people pressed closer round us. Those in the foremost rank threw up their arms in the air, stretched them towards the elephant, bowed down, knelt, cast themselves prostrate on the ground, and distinctly manifested the most profound adoration.

There we stood beneath the verandah, very anxious to know what this display of fanaticism would lead to. McNeil joined us, and looked on in silence. Banks took his place with Storr in the howdah, from which he could direct every movement of Behemoth.

By four o'clock steam was up. The noise made by the engine was, of course, taken by the Hindoos for the angry trumpeting of an elephant belonging to a supernatural race. Storr allowed the steam to escape by the valves, and it appeared to issue from the sides, and through the skin of the gigantic quadruped.

"We are at high pressure."

"Go ahead, Banks," returned the colonel; "but be careful; don't let us crush anybody."

It was almost day. The road along the river bank was

occupied by this great crowd of devotees, who seemed to have no idea of making way for us, so that to go forward and crush no one was anything but easy. The steam-whistle gave forth two or three short piercing shrieks, to which the pilgrims replied by frantic howls.

"Clear the way there!" shouted the engineer, telling the stoker at the same time to open the regulator. The steam bellowed as it rushed into the cylinders; the wheels made half a revolution, and a huge jet of white smoke issued from the trunk.

For an instant the crowd swerved aside. The regulator was then half open; the trumpeting and snorting of Behemoth increased in vehemence, and our train began to advance between the serried ranks of the natives, who seemed loth to give place to it.

"Look out, Banks!" I suddenly exclaimed.

I was leaning over the verandah rails, and I beheld a dozen of these fanatics cast themselves on the road, with the evident wish to be crushed beneath the wheels of the monstrous machine.

"Stand back there! Attention!" shouted Colonel Munro, signing to them to rise.

"Oh, the idiots!" cried Captain Hood; "they take us for the car of Juggernaut! They want to get pounded beneath the feet of the sacred elephant!"

At a sign from Banks, the fireman shut off steam. The

pilgrims, lying across the road, seemed desirous not to move. The fanatic crowd around them uttered loud cries, and appeared by their gestures to encourage them to persevere.

The engine was at a standstill. Banks was excessively embarrassed.

All at once an idea struck him.

"Now we shall see!" he cried; and turning the tap of the clearance pipes under the boiler, strong jets of steam issued forth, and spread along the surface of the ground; while the air was filled by the shrill, harsh screams of the whistle.

"Hurrah! hurrah!" shouted Captain Hood. "Give it them, Banks! give it them well!"

The method proved successful. As the streams of vapour reached the fanatics, they sprang up with loud cries of pain. They were prepared and anxious to be run over, but not to be scalded.

The crowd drew back. The way was clear. Steam was put on in good earnest, and the wheels revolved steadily.

"Forward!" exclaimed Captain Hood, clapping his hands and laughing heartily.

And at a rapid rate Behemoth took his way along the road, vanishing in a cloud of vapour, like some mysterious visitant, from before the eyes of the wondering crowd.

CHAPTER VIII.

A FEW HOURS AT BENARES.

THE high road now lay open before our Steam House, a road which *viâ* Sasseram, would lead us along the right bank of the Ganges, up to Benares.

A mile beyond the encampment our engine slackened its speed, and we proceeded at the more moderate pace of about seven miles and a half an hour. It was Banks' intention to camp that evening seventy-five miles from Gaya, and to pass the night quietly in the neighbourhood of the little town of Sasseram.

In general Indian roads avoid watercourses as much as possible, for they necessitate bridges, which are very expensive affairs to erect on that alluvial soil. In many places where it was found impossible to prevent a river or stream from barring the path, there is no means of transit except an ancient and clumsy ferry-boat, of no use for the conveyance of our train. Fortunately, however, we were independent.

We had that very day to cross an important river, the Sone. This stream is fed above Rhotas by its affluents the Coput and the Coyle, and flows into the Ganges just between Arrah and Dinapore.

Nothing could be easier than our passage. The elephant took to the water quite naturally. It descended the gentle slope of the bank straight into the river, rested on the surface, and with its huge feet beating the water like a paddle-wheel, it quietly drew our floating train to the opposite bank.

Captain Hood could not contain his delight.

"A travelling house!" he would exclaim, "a house which is both a carriage and a steamboat. Now we only need wings to enable us to fly through the air, and thus to cleave space."

"That will be done some day or other, Hood," rejoined the engineer, quite seriously.

"I believe it, Banks," answered the captain, no less seriously. "It will be done! But what can't be done, is that our life should be given back to us a couple of hundred years hence to enable us to see all these marvels! Life is not all sunshine, but yet I would willingly consent to live ten centuries out of pure curiosity!"

That evening, twelve hours after leaving Gaya, we passed under the magnificent tubular railway bridge, eighty feet above the bed of the Sone, and encamped in

A FEW HOURS AT BENARES.

the environs of Sasseram. We merely wished to spend a night in this spot, to replenish our stock of wood and water, and start again at dawn of day.

This programme we carried out, and next morning, before the burning mid-day heat began, we were far on our way.

The landscape was still much the same; that is, very rich and very cultivated. Such it appeared on approaching the marvellous valley of the Ganges. I will not stop to describe the numberless villages we passed lying in the midst of extensive rice-fields, nestling amid groves of palms, interspersed with mangoes and other trees of magnificent growth and foliage.

We never paused on our way; for even if the road was blocked by a cart, drawn by slow-paced zebus, two or three shrieks from our whistle caused them to draw on one side, and we dashed past to the great amazement of the ryots.

I was delighted and charmed at the sight of a great number of fields of roses. We were indeed not far distant from Ghazipore, the great centre of production of the water, or rather essence, made from these flowers.

I asked Banks if he could give me any information about this most valued product, which in the matter of perfumery seems to be the height of perfection.

"Here is a calculation," was Bank's reply, "which will

show you at once what a costly manufacture it is. Forty pounds of roses are first of all subjected to a sort of slow distillation over a gentle fire, and the whole yields about thirty pounds of rose-water. This is thrown on to another heap of forty pounds of flowers, which in its turn is distilled until the mixture is reduced to twenty pounds. This is then exposed to the cool night air for twelve hours, and the next day is found congealed on the surface—how much do you think?—one ounce of sweet-scented oil! So then, out of eighty pounds of roses— a quantity which they say contains not less than two hundred thousand flowers—is finally obtained but one ounce of liquid. Is it not a regular massacre? Therefore it is not astonishing that, even in the country where it is made, the attar of roses should cost forty rupees, or four pounds the ounce."

"Well!" ejaculated Captain Hood, "if it required eighty pound of grapes to make one ounce of brandy, grog would soon become a costly beverage!"

We now crossed the Karamanca, one of the affluents of the Ganges. The Hindoos have made of this poor innocent river a sort of Styx, and believe it very unlucky and unsafe for navigation. Its banks are no less accursed than those of the Dead Sea. Bodies which are entrusted to it are carried straight to the Brahminical hell. I will not discuss these beliefs; but as to admitting that the water of this diabolical river is disagreeable to the taste or unwholesome, I protest against it, and assert that it is excellent.

That evening, having traversed a tolerably level country between immense fields of poppies and tracts of rice marked out like a chess-board, we camped on the right bank of the Ganges, before the ancient Jerusalem of the Hindoos—the sacred city of Benares.

"Twenty-four hours' halt here," said Banks.

"At what distance from Calcutta are we now?" I asked the engineer."

"About three hundred and fifty miles," he replied; "and you acknowledge, my friend, do you not, that we have felt nothing of the length of the way or the fatigue of the journey."

The Ganges! Is not that a name which calls up the most poetic legends, and does it not seem as if all India was summed up in that word? Is there in the world a valley to be compared to this, extending over a space of fifteen hundred miles, and containing not less than a hundred million inhabitants? Is there a spot on the globe where more wonders have been heaped up since the appearance of the Asiatic races? What would not Victor Hugo have said of the Ganges, when he has so proudly sung the Danube? Yes, a river is worth something which can say of itself that it has—

> "Comme une mer sa houle,
> Quand sur le globe on déroule
> Comme un serpent, et quand on roule
> De l'occident à l'orient!"

But the Ganges has billows and cyclones, more terrible than the storms of the European river! The Ganges winds like a serpent through the most poetic countries in the world! And the Ganges flows from west to east! But it is in no ordinary range of hills that it takes its source! It flows from the highest chain in the globe, from the mountains of Thibet, and dashes down, absorbing all its tributaries on the way. It is among the Himalayas themselves that it springs into being.

When we looked out the next morning, the 23rd of May, the rising sun was shining on the sheet of water spread out before our eyes. Several alligators of great size lay on the white sand, as if drinking in the early sunlight. Motionless, they were turned towards the radiant orb, as if they had been the most faithful votaries of Brahma. But the sight of several corpses floating by aroused them from their adoration.

It is said that these bodies float on the back when they are men, and on the chest when they are women, but from personal observation I can state that there is no truth in this statement. In a moment the monsters had darted on the prey, daily furnished to them on the waters of these rivers, and with it plunged into the depths.

The Calcutta railway, before branching off at Allahabad to run towards Delhi, keeps close to the right bank of the Ganges, although it does not follow the river in all its numerous windings. At the Mogul-Serai station, from which we were but a few miles distant, a small branch line turns off, which passes Benares by crossing the river, and, passing through the valley of the Goumtie, reaches Jaunpore at a distance of about thirty-five miles.

Benares lies on the left bank. But it was at Allahabad, and not here, that we were to cross the Ganges. Our Behemoth stood therefore in the encampment we had chosen on the evening of the 22nd of May. Several boats were moored to the bank, ready to take us across to the sacred town, which I was very desirous of exploring carefully.

These cities had been so often visited by Colonel Munro that there was really nothing new to him to learn or see in this one. He had, however, at first thought of accompanying us that day; but on reflection, decided to make an excursion along the banks of the river instead, with Sergeant McNeil as his companion; so the two quitted Steam House before we ourselves had started. Captain Hood had at one time been quartered at Benares, and he was anxious to go and see a few of his old friends there. Banks and I, therefore—the engineer having expressed a wish to be my guide—were the only members of our party whom a feeling of curiosity attracted to the city.

When I say that Captain Hood had once been quartered at Benares, it must be understood that the English troops are not usually quartered in Hindoo towns. Their barracks are situated in cantonments, which in reality become regular English towns. Such is the case at Allahabad, Benares, and several other places in the country; where not only soldiers, but officials, merchants, and gentlemen, live by preference. Each of these great cities has, therefore, a double, one possessing all the comforts of modern Europe, the other having preserved the customs of the country, and the Hindoo usages, in all their local colour.

The English town annexed to Benares is called Secrole, and its bungalows, avenues, and Christian churches, are not particularly interesting to visit. Here, too, are found the principal hotels frequented by tourists. Secrole is one of those ready-made cities which the manufacturers of the United Kingdom can send out in boxes ready to be set up on the premises; it therefore presents nothing curious. Banks and I embarked in a boat and crossed the Ganges obliquely, so as to get a beautiful view of the magnificent amphitheatre in which Benares lies.

"Benares," said Banks, "is the most holy city of India. It is the Hindoo Mecca, and whoever has lived in it, if only for four-and-twenty hours, is assured of eternal happiness. One can imagine, then, what an enormous crowd of pilgrims such a belief would attract thither, and what a great population must reside in a city for which Brahma has reserved blessings of such importance."

Benares is supposed to have existed for more than thirty centuries, and must therefore have been founded about the time when Troy disappeared. It always exercised a great influence—not political, but spiritual—over Hindoostan, and was the authorized centre of the Buddhist religion until the ninth century. A religious revolution then occurred. Brahminism destroyed the ancient worship. Benares became the Brahmin capital, the centre of attraction to the faithful, and it is said that 300,000 pilgrims visit it annually.

The Holy City still has its Rajah. Though he is a stipendiary of the British, and his salary is somewhat poor, he is still a prince, and inhabits a magnificent residence at Ramnagur, on the Ganges. He is a veritable descendant of the kings of Kaci, the ancient name of Benares, but has no real influence; though he would console himself for that if his pension had not been reduced to a lac of rupees, which is 100,000 rupees, or 10,000*l*.; only enough for the pocket-money of a Nabob in the old times.

Benares, like all towns in the valley of the Ganges, took part in the great insurrection of 1857. Its garrison was at this time composed of the 37th regiment of native infantry, a corps of irregular cavalry, and half a Sikh regiment. The English troops consisted merely of a half battery of artillery. This handful of men could not attempt to disarm the native soldiers. The authorities therefore waited with impatience for the arrival of Colonel Neil, who set out for Allahabad with the 10th regiment. Colonel Neil entered Benares with only 250 men, and gave orders for a parade on the drill-ground.

When all were assembled, the sepoys were told to give up their arms. They refused. A fight then ensued between them and Colonel Neil's infantry. The irregular cavalry almost immediately joined the mutineers, as did the Sikhs, who believed themselves betrayed.

The half battery, however, opened fire on them, and notwithstanding that they fought with valour and desperation, all were put to the rout.

This fight took place outside the town. Inside there was an attempt at insurrection on the part of the Mussulmans, who hoisted the green flag, but this was soon quelled. From that time, and throughout the rest of the revolt, Benares was troubled no more, even at the time when the insurrection appeared triumphant in the provinces of the west.

These details Banks gave me as our boat glided slowly over the water of the Ganges.

"My dear fellow," he remarked, "you are now going to pay your first visit to Benares. But although this city is so ancient, you must not expect to find in it any monument more than three hundred years old. Don't be astonished at this. It is the consequence of those religious contests in which fire and sword has played such a lamentable part. But all the same, Benares is a very remarkable and curious town, and you will not regret an excursion to it."

We now stopped our boat at a suitable distance to allow us to gaze across a bay as blue as that of Naples, at the picturesque amphitheatre of terraced houses and palaces descending to the water's edge, some of them projecting over the river, so that the waves constantly washed their base and appeared likely some day to undermine them. A pagoda of Chinese architecture, consecrated to Buddha—a perfect forest of towers, spires, and minarets—beautified the city, studded as it is with mosques and temples, the latter surmounted by the Lingam, one of the symbols of Siva, whilst the lofty Mohammedan mosque built by Aurungzebe, crowned the marvellous panorama.

Instead of disembarking at one of the "ghâts," or flights of stone steps leading from the banks of the river up to the terraces, Banks directed the boatman to take us first past the quay.

Here I found the scene at Gaya reproduced, though with

a different landscape. Instead of the green forests of the Phalgou, we had this holy city for a background. But the life part of the picture was much the same.

Thousands of pilgrims covered the banks, the terraces, the stairs, and devoutly plunged into the stream, in rows of three or four deep. It must not be imagined that this bath was free. Sentries in red turbans, with sabres at their sides, stood on the lower steps of the ghâts, and exacted tribute, in company with industrious brahmins, who sold chaplets, amulets, charms, and other religious articles.

But besides the pilgrims who bathed on their own account, there were also traders whose only business was to draw this most sacred water, and transport it to the distant parts of the peninsula. As a security, each phial is marked with the seal of the Brahmins. But in spite of this, fraud is carried on to a great extent, as the exportation of this miraculous liquid is so considerable.

"Perhaps," as Banks said to me, "all the water of the Ganges would not be sufficient to supply the wants of the faithful."

I asked if these bathers did not often meet with accidents, for no one seemed to try to prevent such a thing. There were no swimmers to prevent imprudent people from venturing too far into the rapid current.

"Accidents are indeed frequent," answered Banks; "but

if the body of the devotee is lost, his soul is saved; therefore they do not concern themselves much about it."

"And crocodiles?" I added.

"Crocodiles," replied Banks, "usually keep their distance. All this noise terrifies them. These monsters are not to be feared so much as villains who dive under the water, seize women and children, and tear off their jewels. There is even a story about one of these wretches, who, by means of an artificial head, played the part of a crocodile for a long time, and made quite a little fortune by this profitable though dangerous trade. Finally, this impertinent intruder was devoured one day by a real alligator, and nothing was found of him but his head of tanned skin, floating on the surface of the water.

"There are also desperate fanatics who voluntarily seek death in the depths of the Ganges; and this they do with a curious species of refinement. Round their body they tie a chaplet of open but empty urns; gradually the water fills these vessels, and the devotee gently sinks down, amid the applause of the crowd."

Our boat at last landed us at the Manmenka Ghât. Here were arranged in layers the funeral piles on which the corpses of all those who in their lifetime had had any care for their future existence, were burnt. In this sacred spot, cremation is eagerly sought for by the faithful, and these funeral piles burn night and day. Rich baboos of distant territories cause themselves to be carried to Benares as soon as they are attacked by an illness which they feel will prove fatal. Benares is unquestionably the best starting-point for a journey to the other world. If the deceased has only to reproach himself with venial faults, his soul is wafted on the smoke of the Manmenka straight to the regions of eternal bliss. If, on the contrary, he has been a great sinner, his soul must go and inhabit the body of a Brahmin yet to be born, for the purpose of being regenerated. It is to be hoped that his second life will be exemplary, or he will be exposed to a third trial before he is finally admitted to share the delights of Brahma's heaven.

The rest of the day we devoted to exploring the town, its principal monuments, and its bazaars, lined with dark shops after the Arab fashion. Here they sold principally fine muslin of beautiful texture, and "kinkob," a rich silk material, brocaded with gold, which is one of the principal products of the Benares industry. The streets were clean, but so narrow as almost to prevent the sun's rays from penetrating to the pavement. But although it was shady, the heat was stifling. I pitied the bearers of our palanquin, who yet seemed to make no complaint themselves.

However, it being an opportunity for the poor wretches to earn a few rupees was sufficient to give them strength and spirit. But a certain Hindoo, or rather Bengalee, with a keen eye and cunning expression, had no such reason for following us, as he did, the whole day, and without much attempt at concealment. As we landed at the Manmenka Ghât, I had been speaking to Banks, and uttered aloud the name of Colonel Munro. The Bengalee, who was watching our boat put in, gave an evident start. I did not at the time pay much attention to this, but recalled the circumstance when I perceived the spy incessantly dogging our steps. He only left us to appear again, either before or behind, a few minutes later. Whether friend or foe I could not tell, but that he was a man to whom the name of Colonel Munro was not indifferent was perfectly evident.

Our palanquin soon stopped at the foot of a staircase of a hundred steps, leading from the quay to the mosque of Aurungzebe.

Formerly the devotees only ascended these Santa Scala on their knees, after the manner of the faithful at Rome; but that was when a magnificent Hindoo temple dedicated to Vishnu was on the site now occupied by the mosque of the conqueror.

I should much have liked to survey Benares from the top of one of the minarets of this mosque, the construction of which is regarded as a perfect triumph of architecture. Although 132 feet in height, they have scarcely the diameter of a manufactory chimney, and yet the cylindrical shaft contains a winding stair. No one is allowed to ascend, and there is a reason for this prohibition: the two minarets are already sensibly out of the perpendicular, and unless endowed with the vitality of the Tower of Pisa, they will end by coming down some day.

On leaving the mosque of Aurungzebe, I found the Bengalee waiting for us at the door. This time I looked fixedly at him, and he lowered his eyes. Before drawing Bank's attention to this incident, I wished to ascertain if this individual would persist in his suspicious behaviour, and for the present I said nothing.

You may count pagodas and mosques by hundreds in this marvellous town of Benares. Also splendid palaces— the most beautiful of which is unquestionably that of the King of Nagpore. Few rajahs indeed neglect to secure a house in the Holy City, and always come to it at the time of the great religious festivals of Mela.

I could not attempt to visit all these buildings during the little time we had at our disposal, I contented myself, therefore, with making a visit to the temple of Bicheshwar, in which is set up the Lingam of Siva. This—a shapeless stone, looked upon as part of the body of this the most savage god of the Hindoo mythology—covers a well the stagnant waters of which possess, they say, miraculous virtues. I saw also the Mankarnika, or sacred fountain, where devotees bathe, to the great profit of the Brahmins;

then the Manmundir, an observatory built two hundred years ago by the Emperor Akbar.

I had heard of a palace of monkeys, which all tourists never failed to visit. A Parisian naturally imagined himself about to behold something like the celebrated monkey-house in the Jardin des Plantes. But there was nothing of the sort. I found that this palace was a temple, called the Dourga-Khound, situated a little beyond the outskirts, The monkeys were by no means shut up in cages. They roamed freely through the courts, leaping from wall to wall, climbing to the tops of enormous mango-trees, noisily disputing over the parched corn brought by their visitors, and to which they are very partial.

There, as everywhere else, the Brahmins, who keep the Dourga-Khound, levy a small contribution, which evidently makes this profession one of the most lucrative in India.

It is needless to say that we were rather done up by the heat, as towards evening we began to think of returning to Steam House. We had breakfasted and dined at Secrole, in one of the best hotels of that English town, and yet I must say that the cuisine made us regret that of Monsieur Parazard.

As we were stepping into our boat to return to the right bank of the Ganges, I again caught sight of the Bengalee a short distance from us. A skiff containing a Hindoo was waiting for him, into which he got. Did he mean to cross the river, and so follow us to our encampment? This looked suspicious.

"Banks," said I in a low tone, pointing to the Bengalee, "that fellow is a spy, who has followed us every step of the way. . . ."

"I have seen him," returned Banks; "and I also noticed that it was the colonel's name, uttered by you, which first put him on the alert."

"Isn't there any . . . ?" I said.

"No; leave him alone," said Banks. "Better not to let him know that he is suspected. . . . Besides, he has gone now."

In fact, the Bengalee's canoe had already disappeared amongst the numerous vessels of all shapes and sizes, covering the dark waters of the Ganges.

Banks turned to our boatman.

"Do you know that man?" he asked, in a tone of affected indifference.

"No; this is the first time I have seen him," replied the native.

Night fell. Hundreds of boats, dressed with flags illuminated with many-coloured lanterns, and filled with singers and instrumentalists, glided here and there over the surface of the water. From the left bank rose beautiful and varied fireworks, reminding me that we were not far from the Celestial Empire, where they are held in such favour. It would be difficult to give a description of this really matchless spectacle. Of course we could not tell for what reason, or in whose honour, this night-festival was held, but all classes of the Hindoos took part in it. Just as it ended, our boat touched the opposite bank.

It was like a dream. These beautiful and ephemeral fires illuminated space for a moment, and then died away in the blackness of night. But, as I said before, India worships three hundred millions of gods, demi-gods, saints, and demi-saints, of every kind and description, so that the year has not enough hours, minutes, or seconds, to devote even one to each of their divinities.

On reaching our encampment, we found Colonel Munro and Sergeant McNeil already there. Banks asked the sergeant if anything had happened during our absence.

"Nothing," was the reply.

"You haven't seen any suspicious-looking person prowling about?"

"No, Mr. Banks. Have you any reason for suspecting . . . ?"

"We have been dogged during our excursion in Benares," answered the engineer, "and I did not like the look of the fellow who followed us!"

"The spy was . . . ?"

"A Bengalee, who was put on the alert by the mention of Colonel Munro's name."

"What could the man want with us?"

"I don't know, McNeil. We must keep a look out."

"We will!" returned the sergeant emphatically.

CHAPTER IX.

ALLAHABAD.

THE distance between Benares and Allahabad is about eighty miles, and the road lies on the right bank of the Ganges between the railway and the river. Storr had loaded the tender with a good supply of coal, so that the elephant would have no lack of nourishment for several days. Well cleaned—I had almost said well curry-combed—as bright as if he had just come out of the workshop, he impatiently waited the moment for starting. He didn't exactly paw the ground, but the quivering of the wheels betrayed the tension of the steam which filled his lungs of steel.

Our train started early in the morning of the 24th, at a rate of three to four miles an hour.

The night passed quietly, and we saw nothing of the Bengalee.

I may as well mention here, once for all, that each day's programme, of getting up, going to bed, breakfasts, luncheons, dinners, and siestas, was carried out with military exactitude. Our life in the Steam House went on as regularly as in the bungalow at Calcutta. The landscape was constantly changing under our eyes, without any perceptible movement of our house. We soon grew accustomed to our life, as do passengers on board an ocean steamer, though we had nothing monotonous, for, unlike the sea, our horizon was ever changing.

Towards eleven o'clock we caught sight, on the plain, of a curious mausoleum, erected in honour of two holy personages of Islam, "Cassim-Soliman," father and son. Half-an-hour after this we passed the important fortress of Chunar, an impregnable rock crowned by picturesque ramparts, and rising perpendicularly 150 feet above the river.

Of course we halted to pay this place a visit, as it is one of the most important fortresses in the valley of the Ganges.

It is a very economical place with regard to expenditure of powder and bullets, for when an assaulting column endeavours to scale the walls, it is immediately crushed by an avalanche of rocks and stones kept for the purpose.

At its foot lies the town which bears its name, the houses coquettishly peeping out from among the verdure.

In Benares, as we have seen, there exist many privileged places, which are considered by the Hindoos as the most sacred in the world. If one began to count, the number scattered over the peninsula would amount to

ALLAHABAD.

hundreds. Chunar possesses one of these miraculous spots. Here you are shown a marble slab, to which some god or other comes regularly to take his daily siesta. It is true that he is invisible, so we did not stop to see him.

That evening Behemoth halted near Mirzapore to pass the night. This town has no lack of temples, and has also manufactories and a wharf, from which vessels are laden with the cotton grown in that territory. It will some day become a rich commercial city.

About two o'clock next day we forded the little river Tonsa, at that time only containing a foot of water. Then, five hours after, we passed the point where the great branch line from Bombay to Calcutta joins the main railway, near the place where the Jumna falls into the Ganges. We admired the magnificent iron viaduct, its sixteen piers, sixty feet in height, washed by the waters of this superb confluent. We had to cross this river by means of a bridge of boats, over half-a-mile in length, which we accomplished without much difficulty, and by the evening were encamped at the end of one of the suburbs of Allahabad.

The 26th we devoted to visiting this important town, which is a junction of all the principal railways in Hindoostan. Its situation is admirable, in the midst of a rich territory, between the two arms of the Jumna and Ganges.

Nature certainly has done everything in her power to fit

Allahabad to be the capital of British India, the centre of Government, and residence of the Viceroy; and it is not impossible that it will one day become so, if the cyclones play enough mischief with Calcutta, the actual metropolis. Some clever heads must already have foreseen this contingency, for in this great body called India Allahabad is placed where the heart should be, just as Paris is the heart of France. London is not in the centre of the United Kingdom, it is true; but then London has not the same pre-eminence over other great English cities such as Liverpool, Manchester, Birmingham, that Paris has over all the other towns in France.

"And starting from here," said I to Banks, "shall we proceed in a straight and northerly direction?"

"Yes," replied Banks, "or rather, almost straight; Allahabad being the western limit of this, the first part of our expedition.

"After all," cried Captain Hood, "these great towns are very well in their way, but give me an open plain or a tangled jungle! If we always keep near railways like this, we shall end by running on them ourselves, and our Behemoth will be turned into a common engine. What a come-down!"

"Cheer up; don't be uneasy, Hood, "returned the engineer; "that won't happen. We shall soon venture into your favourite parts."

"Then, Banks, do we make straight for the Indo-Chinese frontier, without going through Lucknow?"

"My advice is that we should avoid that town, and more especially Cawnpore, a place so full of terrible recollections for Colonel Munro."

"You are right," I replied; "we can't keep too far away from it!"

"I say, Banks," asked Captain Hood, "didn't you hear anything about Nana Sahib during your visit to Benares?"

"Nothing," answered the engineer. "It is very probable that the Governor of Bombay may have been misled, and that the Nana never reappeared in the presidency of Bombay."

"That is very likely," answered the captain, "otherwise the old rebel would already have made himself talked of!"

"However that may be," said Banks, "I am anxious to leave the Ganges valley; it has been the scene of so many disasters during the sepoy mutiny, from Allahabad up to Cawnpore. But we must be especially careful that neither the latter town nor the name of Nana Sahib should be mentioned before the colonel. Do not let us awake painful recollections."

On the next day Banks again wished to accompany me during the few hours I was able to spend in Allahabad.

One might easily have spent three days in exploring the three towns of which it is composed, but it is less curious than Benares, although numbered among the holy cities.

There is really nothing to say about the Hindoo part of the town. It is simply a mass of low houses, separated by narrow streets, shaded by magnificent tamarind-trees.

Of the English town and cantonments, there is not much to be said either. The fine well-planted avenues, wealthy habitations, and wide squares, all look as if the town was destined to become a great capital.

Allahabad is situated in a vast plain, bounded on the north and south by the double course of the Jumna and Ganges. It is called the "Plain of Almsgiving," because the Hindoo princes have at all times come here to perform works of charity. M. Rousselet, quoting a passage from the "Life of Hionen Thsang," says, "It is more meritorious to give away one piece of money in this place, than a hundred thousand elsewhere."

Now for a few words about the fort of Allahabad, which is well worth a visit. It is constructed to the west of the great Almsgiving plain, from which its high granite walls stand boldly out. In the middle of the fort is a palace, now used as an arsenal, though formerly the favourite residence of the Sultan Akbar. In one of the corners is the Lat of Feroze Schachs, a superb monolith thirty-six feet in height supporting a lion. Not far off is a little temple, which no

ALLAHABAD. 147

Hindoo can visit, as they are refused admission into the fort, although it is one of the most sacred places in the world. Such are the principal objects of interest.

Banks told me that the fort of Allahabad also has its legend, which reminds one of the story relative to the reconstruction of Solomon's temple in Jerusalem. When the Sultan wished to build this fort, it seems that the stones turned very refractory. Directly a wall was built, it tumbled itself down again. The oracle was consulted. The oracle replied, as usual, that a voluntary victim must be offered to remove this spell.

A Hindoo offered himself as a holocaust; he was sacrificed, and the fort was soon finished. This man was called Brog, and that is the reason why the town is still designated by the double name of Brog-Allahabad.

Banks took us to the deservedly celebrated gardens of Khousroo. Here numerous Mohammedan mausoleums stand under the shade of beautiful tamarinds. One of them is the last resting-place of the sultan from whom these gardens take their name. On one of the white marble walls is printed the palm of an enormous hand. This was pointed out to us with a complacency which was lacking in the exhibition of the sacred impressions at Gaya.

It is true this was not the print of a god's foot, but that of the hand of a simple mortal, the great nephew of Mahomet. During the insurrection of 1857, blood flowed as freely in Allahabad as in the other towns of the Ganges valley. The fight between the English and the mutineers on the drill-ground at Benares caused the rising of the native troops, and in particular the revolt of the 6th regiment of the Bengal army. Eight ensigns were massacred to begin with; but thanks to the energetic conduct of some European artillerymen who were at Chunar, the sepoys ended by laying down their arms.

It was a more serious affair in the cantonments. The natives rose, threw open the prisons, pillaged the docks, and set fire to the European houses. In the midst of all this, Colonel Neil, who had re-established order at Benares, arrived with his own regiment and a hundred fusiliers belonging to a Madras regiment. He retook the bridge of boats, seized the suburbs of the town, dispersed the members of a provisional government installed by a Mussulman, and very soon again became master of the province.

During our short excursions in Allahabad, Banks and I carefully watched to see if we were followed there as we had been in Benares, but saw nothing to arouse our suspicions.

"Never mind," said the engineer, "we must all the same be on our guard. I should have liked to have travelled incognito, for Colonel Munro's name is too well known among the natives of this province."

At six o'clock we returned to dinner. Sir Edward, who

had left the encampment for an hour or two, had also come back, and was waiting for us, as was Captain Hood, who had been visiting some of his old comrades in the cantonment.

I observed to Banks that Colonel Munro seemed not more sad, but more anxious than was his wont. There appeared in his eyes a latent fire that tears should surely long ago have extinguished.

"You are right," answered Banks; "there is something the matter. What can have happened?"

"Suppose you ask McNeil?" said I.

"Ah, yes, perhaps he will know."

And leaving the drawing-room, the engineer opened the door of the sergeant's cabin.

He was not there.

"Where is McNeil?" asked Banks of Goûmi, who was getting ready to wait at table.

"He has left the camp," replied Goûmi.

"How long?"

"He went nearly an hour ago, by Colonel Munro's orders."

"You do not know where he has gone?"

"No, sahib, and I cannot tell why he went."

"Nothing fresh has happened here since we left?"

"Nothing, sahib."

Banks returned, and telling me of the sergeant's absence for a reason that no one knew, he repeated,—

"I do not know what it is, but very certainly there is something up. We must wait and see."

Every one now sat down to table. Ordinarily, Colonel Munro took part in the conversation during meals. He liked to hear us relate our adventures and excursions, and was interested in all we had been doing during the day.

I always took care to avoid speaking of anything that could in the slightest degree remind him of the mutiny. I think that he perceived this; but whether he appreciated it or not, it was sometimes difficult enough to maintain this reserve, especially when we talked of towns such as Benares and Allahabad.

During dinner, on the evening of which I speak, I feared being obliged to speak of Allahabad. I need not have been afraid, however. Colonel Munro questioned neither Banks nor myself about the occupation of our day. He remained mute during the whole of dinner, and as time went on his preoccupation visibly increased. He cast frequent glances along the road which led to the cantonments, and several times was evidently on the point of rising from table, the better to see in that direction. It was plain that he was impatiently awaiting the return of Sergeant McNeil.

Our meal was dull enough. Hood looked interrogatively at Banks, as if to ask him what was the matter, but Banks knew no more than he did.

When dinner at last came to an end, Colonel Munro, instead of as usual lying down to take a nap, stepped down from the verandah, went a few paces along the road, gave one long look down it ; then, returning towards us,—

"Banks, Hood, and you too, Maucler," he said, "will you accompany me as far as the nearest houses of the cantonments?"

We all immediately rose and followed the colonel, who walked slowly on without uttering a word.

After proceeding thus for about a hundred paces, Sir Edward stopped before a post standing on the right hand side of the road, and having a notice stuck on it.

"Read that," he said.

It was the placard, already more than two months old, which put a price on the head of Nana Sahib, and gave notice of his presence in the presidency of Bombay.

Banks and Hood could scarcely conceal their disappointment. While still in Calcutta, and during the journey, they had so managed, up to the present time, that this notice had never come under the colonel's eyes. But now a vexatious chance had baffled all their precautions.

"Banks!" said Sir Edward, seizing the engineer's hand, "did you know of this notice?"

Banks made no reply.

"You knew two months ago," continued the colonel,

"of this announcement that Nana Sahib was in the presidency of Bombay, and yet you said nothing to me."

Banks remained silent, not knowing what to say.

"Well, yes, colonel," exclaimed Captain Hood, "we did know of it, but what was the use of telling you? Who was to prove that the fact announced by this notice is true, and what was the good of bringing to your mind those painful recollections which do you so much harm?"

"Banks," cried Colonel Munro, his face as it were, transformed, "have you forgotten that it is my right, that I of all men must do justice on that wretch? Know this! when I consented to leave Calcutta, I did so, because this journey would take me to the north of India, because I never even for a single day believed in the death of Nana Sahib, and because I will never relinquish my purpose of vengeance. In setting out with you, I had but one idea, one hope. For the attainment of my purpose, on the chances of the journey, and the aid of heaven, I had relied. I was right in so doing. Heaven directed me to this notice. It is in the south, and not in the north, that Nana Sahib must be sought for. Be it so; I shall go south."

We had not been mistaken in our fears. It was but too true. A fancy—nay more, a fixed idea—still governed the mind of Colonel Munro. He had just disclosed it to us.

"Munro," returned Banks, "if I said nothing to you about this, it was because I did not believe in Nana Sahib's being in the Bombay presidency. It is probable that the authorities have been once more mistaken. In fact, that notice is dated the 6th of March, and since that time nothing has been heard to corroborate the statement of the appearance of the nabob."

At first Colonel Munro made no answer to the engineer's observation. He took another look along the road, then said,—"My friends, I am about to hear the latest news. McNeil has gone to Allahabad with a letter for the governor. In a few minutes I shall know whether Nana Sahib did indeed reappear in one of the western provinces; whether he is there still, or whether he has again been lost sight of."

"And if he has been seen, if the fact is indisputable, what shall you do, Munro?" asked Banks, grasping the colonel's hand.

"I shall go," replied Sir Edward, "as is my duty, where justice leads me."

"That is positively decided, Munro?"

"Yes, Banks, positively. You must continue your travels without me, my friends. . . . I shall take the train to Bombay this evening."

"But not alone," responded the engineer, turning towards us. "We will accompany you, Munro?"

"Yes, yes, colonel," exclaimed Captain Hood. "We shall certainly not let you go without us. Instead of hunting wild beasts, we will hunt villains."

"Colonel Munro," I added, "will you allow me to join the captain as one of your friends?"

"Yes, Maucler," replied Banks, "this very evening we will leave Allahabad."

"It is needless," said a grave voice behind us.

We all turned, and beheld Sergeant McNeil standing with a newspaper in his hand.

"Read, colonel," said he. "This is what the governor desired me to show you."

Sir Edward took the paper and read as follows:—

"The Governor of the Bombay Presidency requests the public to take notice that the proclamation of the 6th of March, respecting the nabob, Dandou Pant, must now be considered as cancelled. Nana Sahib was yesterday attacked in the defiles of the Sautpourra mountains, where he had taken refuge with his band, and was killed in the skirmish. The body has been identified by the inhabitants of Cawnpore and Lucknow. A finger is wanting on the left hand, and it is known that Nana Sahib had one amputated at the time when his mock obsequies were celebrated to make people believe in his death. The kingdom of India has now nothing further to dread from the machinations of the cruel nabob who has cost her so much blood."

Colonel Munro read these lines in a hollow voice; then the paper fell from his hands.

We remained silent. Nana Sahib's death, now indisputable, delivered us from all fear as to the future.

Colonel Munro said nothing for some minutes, but stood with his hand pressed over his eyes, as if to efface all frightful recollections. Then,—

"When should we leave Allahabad?" he asked.

"To-morrow, at daybreak," replied the engineer.

"Banks," resumed Sir Edward, "could we not stop for a few hours at Cawnpore?"

"You wish it?"

"Yes, Banks, I should like it. . . . I must see Cawnpore once again . . . . for the last time."

"We shall be there in a couple of days," replied the engineer, quietly.

"And after that?" said the colonel.

"After that," answered Banks, "we shall continue our expedition to the north of India."

"Yes, to the north! to the north!" said the colonel, in a tone which stirred me to the depths of my heart.

In truth, it was likely that Sir Edward Munro still entertained some doubt as to the real result of that last skirmish between Nana Sahib and the English. Yet what reason could he have for disbelieving such evidence as this?

The future alone could explain.

CHAPTER X.

VIA DOLOROSA.

THE kingdom of Oude was formerly one of the most important, as it is still one of the richest, provinces in India. It had many sovereigns—some strong, some feeble. The weakness of one of them, named Wajid Ali Shah, brought about the annexation of his kingdom to the dominions of the Company, on the 6th of February, 1857.

This took place only a few months before the outbreak of the insurrection, and it was in Oude that the most frightful massacres were committed, and followed by the most terrible reprisals. The names of two cities remain in mournful celebrity ever since that time: Lucknow and Cawnpore.

Lucknow is the capital; Cawnpore one of the principal towns of the ancient kingdom.

We reached the latter place on the morning of the 29th of May, having followed the right bank of the Ganges through a level plain covered with immense fields of indigo.

For two days we had travelled at a speed of three leagues an hour, and were now nearly 1000 "kilometres" from Calcutta.

Cawnpore is a town of about 60,000 inhabitants. It occupies a strip of land about five miles in length, on the right bank of the Ganges. There is a military cantonment, in which are quartered 7000 men.

The traveller would vainly seek for anything worthy of his attention in this city, although it is of very ancient origin; anterior, they say, to the Christian era. No sentiment of curiosity, then, brought us to Cawnpore. The wishes of Sir Edward alone led us thither.

Early on the morning of the 30th May we quitted our encampment, and Banks, Captain Hood, and I, followed the colonel and Sergeant McNeil along that melancholy route on which the points of mournful interest were for the last time to be revisited.

I will here repeat the facts, as related to me by Banks, which it is necessary should be known.

"Cawnpore, which was garrisoned by reliable troops at the time of the annexation of the kingdom of Oude, contained at the outbreak of the mutiny no more than 250 British soldiers to three regiments of native infantry (the 1st, 53rd, and 56th), two regiments of cavalry, and a battery of Bengal Artillery. There were in the place besides a considerable number of Europeans, workmen, clerks, merchants,

&c., with 850 women and children of the 32nd regiment, which garrisoned Lucknow.

"Colonel Munro had been living at Cawnpore for several years. And it was there he met the lady who became his wife. Miss Hanlay was a charming young Englishwoman, high-spirited, intelligent, and noble-minded, worthy of the love of such a man as the colonel, who adored her. She and her mother resided in a bungalow near Cawnpore, and there, in 1855, she was married to Edward Munro.

"Two years afterwards, in 1857, when the first acts of rebellion occurred at Meerut, Colonel Munro had to rejoin his regiment at a day's notice.

"He was therefore obliged to leave his wife with his mother-in-law at Cawnpore, but thinking that place unsafe, he charged them to make immediate preparations for departure to Calcutta. Alas, his fears were but too surely justified by what followed.

"The departure of Mrs. Hanlay and Lady Munro was delayed, and the consequences were fatal. The unfortunate ladies were unable to leave Cawnpore.

"Sir Hugh Wheeler was then in command of the division— an upright, honourable soldier, who was but too soon to fall a victim to the crafty designs of Nana Sahib.

"The nabob at that time occupied his castle of Bithour, ten miles from Cawnpore, and affected to be on the best possible terms with the Europeans.

"You are aware, my dear Maucler," continued Banks, "that the first outbreak of the insurrection took place at Meerut and Delhi. The news reached Cawnpore on the 4th of May. And on the same day the 1st regiment of sepoys exhibited symptoms of hostility.

"At this moment Nana Sahib came forward with an offer of his services to the Government. General Wheeler was so ill-advised as to place confidence in the good faith of this villain and knave, who immediately sent his own soldiers to occupy the Treasury Buildings.

"That same day an irregular regiment of sepoys, on its way to Cawnpore, mutinied and massacred its British officers at the very gates of the town.

"The danger then became evident in all its magnitude General Wheeler gave orders that all Europeans should take refuge in the barracks, where were quartered the women and children of the 32nd regiment, then at Lucknow. These barracks were situated at the point nearest the road from Allahabad, by which alone succour could arrive.

"It was there that Lady Munro and her mother were shut up; and throughout this imprisonment she manifested the utmost sympathy for her companions in misfortune, tending them with her own hands, assisting them with money, encouraging them by words and example; in short, showing herself to be, as I have told you she was, a noble, heroic woman.

"The arsenal was soon after confided to a guard of the soldiers of Nana Sahib.

"Then the traitor displayed the standard of rebellion; and on the 7th June, the sepoys, at their own desire, attacked the barracks, which was not defended by more than 300 men who could be relied upon.

"They held out bravely, however, against the besiegers' fire, beneath showers of projectiles; suffering sickness of all sorts, dying of hunger and thirst, for the supply of provisions was insufficient, and they had no water, because the wells dried up.

"This resistance lasted until the 27th June.

"Nana Sahib then proposed a capitulation, and General Wheeler committed the unpardonable mistake of signing it, notwithstanding the earnest entreaties of Lady Munro who besought him to continue the contest.

"In consequence of this capitulation, about 500 persons—men, women, and children—Lady Munro and her mother being of the number, were embarked in boats, which were to descend the Ganges, and convey them to Allahabad.

"Scarcely were these unmoored, than the sepoys opened fire; bullets and grape-shot fell upon them like hail. Some of the boats sank, others were burnt; one alone succeeded in passing several miles down the river. In this boat were Lady Munro and her mother, and for an instant they could believe themselves saved. But the soldiers of the Nana pursued, overtook, captured, and brought them back to the cantonments.

"There the prisoners were divided. All the men were put to death at once. The women and children were added to the number of those who had not been massacred on the 27th June. These two hundred victims, for whom protracted agony was reserved, were shut up in a bungalow, the name of which, Bibi-Ghar, will ever be held in sorrowful remembrance."

"How did these horrible details become known to you?" I inquired.

"They were related to me," replied Banks, "by an old sergeant of the 32nd. This man escaped by a miracle, and was sheltered by the Rajah of Raïschwarah, a province of the kingdom of Oude, who received him as well as some other fugitives with the greatest humanity."

"And Lady Munro and her mother?—what became of them?"

"My dear friend," replied Banks, "we have no direct information of what happened, but it is only too easy to conjecture. In fact, the sepoys were masters of Cawnpore, and they were so until the 15th of July, during which period (nineteen days, which were like so many years!) the unhappy victims were in hourly expectation of succour, which only came too late.

"General Havelock was marching from Calcutta to

the relief of Cawnpore, and, after repeatedly defeating the mutineers, he entered it on the 17th of July.

"But two days previously, upon hearing that the British troops had crossed the river Pandou-Naddi, Nana Sahib resolved to signalize the last hours of his occupation of Cawnpore by frightful massacres. No fate seemed to him too severe for the invaders of India.

"Some prisoners, who had shared the captivity of the prisoners at Bibi-Ghar, were brought, and murdered before his eyes.

"The crowd of women and children remained, and among them Lady Munro and her mother.

"A platoon of the 6th regiment of sepoys received orders to fire upon them through the windows of Bibi-Ghar. The execution began, but not being carried out quickly enough to please the Nana, who was about to be compelled to beat a retreat, this sanguinary prince sent for Mussulman butchers to assist the soldiery. It was the butchery of a slaughter-house.

"Next day, the children and women, dead or alive, were flung into a well; and when Havelock's soldiers came up, this well, charged to the brim with corpses, was still reeking!

"Then began the reprisals. A certain number of mutineers, accomplices of Nana Sahib, had fallen into the hands of General Havelock. And the following day he issued that terrible Order of the Day, the terms of which I shall never forget:—

"'The well in which lie the mortal remains of the poor women and children massacred by order of the miscreant Nana Sahib, is to be filled up and carefully covered over in the form of a tomb. A detachment of European British soldiers, under an officer's command, will fulfil the pious duty this evening. But the house and rooms in which the massacre took place are not to be cleansed by the fellow-countrymen of the victims. The officer is to understand that every drop of innocent blood is to be removed by the tongues of the mutineers condemned to die. After having heard the sentence of death, each man is to be conducted to the place of the massacre, and forced to cleanse a portion of the floors. Care must be taken to render the task as repulsive as possible to the religious sentiments of the condemned men, and the lash, if necessary, must not be spared. This being accomplished, the sentence will be carried out on gallows erected near the house.'"

"This," continued Banks, with deep emotion, "was the order for the day. It was executed in all particulars. But it could not restore the lost! And when, two days afterwards, Colonel Munro arrived and sought for tidings or traces of Lady Munro and her mother, he found nothing—nothing!"

All this was related to me by Banks before reaching

Cawnpore. And now it was towards the scene of these horrors that the colonel directed his steps. But first he revisited the bungalow where Lady Munro had lived in her youth, and where he had seen her for the last time.

It was situated a little outside the suburbs, not far from the line of military cantonments.

Nothing of the house remained but ruins, blackened gables, fallen trees decaying on the ground; all was desolation, for the colonel had permitted nothing to be repaired. After the lapse of six years the bungalow remained just as it had been left by the incendiaries.

We spent an hour in this desolate place. Sir Edward moved silently among ruins which awoke so many recollections, sometimes closing his eyes, as if in thought he recalled the happy existence which nothing could ever restore to him.

At length hastily, and as if doing violence to his feelings, he returned to us, and left the house.

We almost began to hope this visit would satisfy him. But no! Sir Edward Munro had resolved to drain to the dregs the bitterness of the sorrow which overwhelmed him in this fatal town.

He wished to go the barracks where his heroic wife had devoted herself so nobly to the care of those who endured there the horrors of a siege.

These barracks stood in the plain outside the town, and

a church was being built on the spot. In order to reach it, we followed a macadamized road shaded by fine trees and among the unfinished new buildings we could distinguish remains of the brick walls which had formed part of the works of defence raised by General Wheeler.[1]

After Colonel Munro had long gazed motionless and in silence upon the ruins of the barracks, he turned to go towards Bibi-Ghar, but Banks, unable to restrain himself, seized his arm, as though to arrest his steps.

Sir Edward looked steadfastly in his face, and said in a terribly calm voice,—

"Let us proceed."

"Munro! I beseech of you!"

"Then I will go alone."

There was no resisting him.

We went towards Bibi-Ghar, which is approached through gardens very well laid out, and planted with fine trees.

[1] This commemorative church has since been completed. It contains marble tablets, on which are inscriptions to the memory of the engineers of the East Indian Railroad, who died of sickness or of their wounds during the great insurrection of 1857; to the memory of officers, non-commissioned officers, and soldiers of the 34th regiment, killed in battle before Cawnpore on the 17th of November; also of Captain Stuart Beatson, and the officers, soldiers, and women of the 32nd regiment, who died during the sieges of Lucknow and of Cawnpore, or during the insurrection; and, lastly, to the memory of the martyrs of Bibi-Ghar, murdered in July, 1857.

The building is of octagonal form, and has a colonnade in gothic style, which surrounds the place where was the well, now filled up and closed in by a casing of stone. This forms a kind of pedestal on which stands a white marble statue representing the Angel of Pity, one of the last works due to the chisel of the sculptor Marochetti.

It was Lord Canning, Governor-General of India during the fearful insurrection of 1857, who caused this monument to be erected. It was constructed from the design of Colonel Yule, of the Engineers, who himself wished to have defrayed all the expenses. Here Sir Edward Munro could no longer restrain his tears. He fell on his knees beside the statue; while Sergeant McNeil, who was close beside him, wept in silence; and we, in the deepest pain, stood looking on, powerless to console this unfathomable grief.

At length Banks, aided by McNeil, succeeded in drawing our friend away from the spot, and I thought of the words traced with his bayonet by one of Havelock's soldiers on the stone brink of the well:—

"Remember Cawnpore!"

CHAPTER XI.

THE MONSOON.

AT eleven o'clock we returned to the encampment, anxious to leave Cawnpore as quickly as possible; but our engine required some trifling repairs, and it was impossible to do so before the following morning.

Part of a day, then, was at my disposal.

I considered that I could not employ it better than by visiting Lucknow, as Banks did not intend to pass through that place, where Colonel Munro would again have been brought in contact with reminiscences of the war. He was right. These vivid recollections were already far too poignant.

At mid-day, then, quitting Steam House, I took the little branch railway which unites Cawnpore to Lucknow.

The distance is not more than twenty leagues, and in a couple of hours I found myself in this important capital of the kingdom of Oude, of which I wished merely to obtain a glance, or, as I might say, an impression.

I soon perceived the truth of what I had heard respecting the great buildings of Lucknow, built during the reigns of the Mohammedan emperors of the seventeenth century.

A Frenchman, named Martin, a native of Lyons, and a common soldier in the army of Lally-Tollendal, became, in 1730, a favourite with the king. He it was who designed, and in fact may be called the architect of the so-called marvels of the capital of Oude.

The Kaiser Bagh, or official residence of the sovereigns, is a whimsical and fantastic medley of every style of architecture which could possibly emanate from the imagination of a corporal, and is a most superficial structure.

The interior is nothing; all the labour has been lavished on the outside, which is at once Hindoo, Chinese, Moorish, and . . . . European.

It is the same with regard to another smaller palace, called the Farid Bakch, which is likewise the work of Martin.

As to the Imâmbara, built in the midst of the fortress by Kaifiatoulla, the greatest architect of India in the seventeenth century, it is really superb, and, bristling with its hundreds of bell-towers, has a grand and imposing effect!

I could not leave Lucknow without seeing the Constantine Palace, which is another of the original performances of the French corporal, and bears his name. I also wished to visit the adjacent garden, called Secunder Bagh, where hundreds of sepoys were executed for having violated the tomb of the humble soldier of fortune before they abandoned the town.

Another French name besides that of Martin is honoured at Lucknow. A non-commissioned officer, formerly of the "Chasseurs d'Afrique," named Duprat, so distinguished himself by his bravery during the mutiny, that the rebels offered to make him their leader. Duprat nobly refused, notwithstanding the promises of wealth held out to tempt him, and the threats with which he was menaced when he stood firm. He remained faithful to the English. But the sepoys, who had failed to make him a traitor, directed against him their special vengeance, and he was slain in an encounter. "Infidel dog!" they had said on his refusal to join them, "we will have thee in spite of thyself!" And they had him; but only when he was dead!

The names of these two French soldiers were united in the reprisals: for the sepoys who had insulted the tomb of the one, and prepared the grave of the other, were ruthlessly put to death!

At length—having admired the magnificent parks which encircle this great city of 500,000 inhabitants as with a belt of verdure and flowers, and having ridden on elephant-back through the principal streets, and the fine boulevard of Hazrat Gaudj—I took the train, and returned to Cawnpore.

Next morning, the 31st of May, we resumed our route.

"Now then!" cried Captain Hood; "we are done at last with your Allahabads, your Cawnpores, Lucknows, and the rest, for which I care about as much as I do for a blank cartridge!"

"Yes, Hood, we have got through all that," replied Banks; "and now for the north, towards which we are to travel almost in a direct line, to the base of the Himalayas."

"Bravo!" resumed the captain. "What I call real India is not the provinces, crammed with native towns and swarming with people, but the region where live in freedom my friends the elephants, lions, tigers, panthers, leopards, bears, bisons, and serpents. That is, in reality, the only habitable part of the whole peninsula! You will see that it is so, Maucler, and you will have no reason to regret the valley of the Ganges!"

"In your society I can regret nothing, my friend," replied I.

"There are, however," said Banks, "some very interesting towns in the north-west; such as Delhi, Agra, and Lahore . . . ."

"Oh! my dear fellow! who ever heard of those miserable little places!" cried Hood.

"Miserable, indeed!" replied Banks. "Let me tell you,

Hood, they are magnificent cities! And," he continued, turning to me, "we must manage to let you see them, Maucler, without throwing out the captain's plans for a sporting campaign."

"All right, Banks," said Hood; "but it is only from to-day that I consider our journey to have fairly commenced."

Presently, in a loud voice, he shouted, "Fox!"

"Here, captain!" answered his servant.

"Fox! get all the guns, rifles, and revolvers in good order!"

"They are so, sir."

"Prepare the cartridges."

"They are prepared."

"Is everything ready?"

"Quite ready, sir."

"Make everything still more ready."

"I will, sir."

"It won't be long before the thirty-eighth takes his place on your glorious list, Fox!"

"The thirty-eighth!" cried the man, with sudden light in his eye; "he won't have to complain of the nice little ball I am keeping ready for him!"

"Get along with you, Fox!"

With a military salute Fox faced about, and re-entered the gun-room.

I will now give an outline of the plan for the second part of our journey—a plan which only unforeseen events were to induce us to alter.

By this route we were to ascend the course of the Ganges towards the north-west for a long way, and then, turning sharp to the north, continue our way between two rivers; one a tributary of the great river, the other of the Goûmi. By this means a considerable number of streams would be avoided; and, passing by Biswah, we should rise in an oblique direction to the lower ranges of the mountains of Nepaul across the western part of Oude and Rohilkund.

This route had been ingeniously planned by Banks, so as to surmount all difficulties. If coal were to fail in the north of Hindoostan, we were sure of having abundance of wood, and Behemoth would easily keep up any rate of speed we wished, on good roads through the grandest forests of the Indian peninsula.

It was agreed that we might easily reach Biswah in six days, allowing for stoppages at convenient places, and time for the sportsmen of the party to exhibit their prowess. Besides, Captain Hood, with Fox and Goûmi, could easily explore the vicinity of the roads, while Behemoth moved slowly along.

I was permitted to join them, although I was far from being an experienced hunter, and I occasionally did so.

I ought to mention that from the moment our journey

took this new aspect, Colonel Munro became more sociable. Once fairly among the plains and forests beyond the valley of the Ganges, he appeared to resume the calm and even tenor of the life he used to lead at Calcutta, although it was impossible to suppose he could forget that we were gradually approaching the north of India, the region whither he was attracted as by an irresistible fatality. His conversation became more animated, both at meals and during the pleasant evening hours when we halted. As for McNeil, he seemed more gloomy than usual. Had the sight of Bibi-Ghar revived his hatred and thirst for vengeance?

"Nana Sahib killed?" said he to me one day. "No, no, sir; they have not done that for us yet!"

The first day of our journey passed without any incident worth recording. Neither Captain Hood nor Fox had a chance of aiming at any sort of animal. It was quite distressing, and so extraordinary that we began to wonder whether the apparition of a steam elephant could be keeping the savage dwellers of the plains at a distance. We passed several jungles, known to be the resort of tigers and other carnivorous feline creatures. Not one showed himself, although the hunters kept away full two miles from us.

They were forced to devote their energies, with Niger and Fan, to shooting for Monsieur Parazard's larder. He expected to be supplied regularly, and considered game for the table of paramount importance, most unreasonably despising the tigers and other beasts Fox talked to him about.

Disdainfully shrugging his shoulders he would ask, "Are they good to eat?"

In the evening we fixed our camp beneath the shelter of a group of enormous banyans.

The night was as tranquil as the day had been calm.

No roars or howlings of wild animals broke the silence. The snorting of Behemoth himself was stilled.

When the camp-fires were extinguished, Banks, to please the captain, refrained from connecting the electric current by which the elephant's eyes would have become two powerful lamps. But nothing came of it. It was the same the two following nights. Hood was getting desperate.

"What can have happened to my kingdom of Oude?" repeated the captain. "It has been translated! There are no more tigers here than in the lowlands of Scotland!"

"Perhaps there may have been 'battues' here lately," suggested Colonel Munro. "The animals may have emigrated *en masse*. But cheer up, my friend, and wait till we reach the foot of the mountains of Nepaul. You will find scope for your hunting instincts there!"

"It is devoutly to be hoped it may be so, colonel," replied Hood, sadly shaking his head. "Otherwise we may as well re-cast our balls, and make small shot of them!"

The 3rd of June was one of the hottest days which we had endured. There was not a breath of wind, and had not the road been shaded by huge trees, I think we must have been literally baked in our rooms. It seemed possible that, in heat like this, wild animals did not care to quit their dens even during the night.

Next morning, at sunrise, the horizon to the westward for the first time appeared somewhat misty. We then had presented to our eyes a magnificent spectacle—the phenomenon of the mirage, which is called in some parts of India "seekote," or castles in the air; and in others "dessasur" or illusion.

What we saw was not a visionary sheet of water, with curious effects of refraction, but a complete chain of low hills, crowned by castles of the most fantastic form, resembling the rocky heights of some Rhenish valley with their ancient fastnesses of the Margraves. In a moment we seemed transported not only to that romantic part of Europe, but into the Middle Ages five or six centuries back.

This phenomenon was surprisingly clear, and gave us a strange sensation of absolute reality. So much so, that the gigantic elephant-engine, with all its apparatus of modern machinery, advancing towards the habitations of men of Europe, in the eleventh century, struck us as far more out of place and unnatural than when traversing, beneath clouds of vapour, the country of Vishnu and Brahma.

"We thank you, fair Lady Nature!" cried Captain Hood; "instead of the minarets and cupolas, mosques and pagodas, we have been accustomed to, you are spreading before us charming old towns and castles of feudal times!"

"How poetical you are this morning, Hood!" returned Banks. "Pray have you been reading romantic ballads lately?"

"Laugh away, Banks; quiz me as much as you like, but just look there! See how objects in the foreground are growing in size! The bushes are turning into trees, the hills into mountains, the—"

"Why the very cats will be tigers soon, won't they, Hood?"

"Ah, Banks! how jolly that would be... There!" continued the captain, "my Rhenish castles are melting away; the town is crumbling to ruins, and we return to realities, seeing only a landscape in the kingdom of Oude, which the very wild animals have deserted."

The sun, rising above the eastern horizon, quickly dissipated the magical effects of refraction. The fortresses, like castles built of cards, sank down with the hills, which were suddenly transformed into plains.

"Well, now that the mirage has vanished, and with it Hood's poetic vein, shall I tell you, my friends," said Banks, "what the phenomenon presages?"

"Say on, great engineer!" quoth the captain.

"Nothing less than a great change of weather," replied Banks. The early days of June are usually marked by climacteric changes. The turn of the monsoon will bring the periodical rainy season."

"My dear Banks," said I, "let it rain as it will, we are snug enough here. Under cover like this I should prefer a deluge to heat such as—"

"All right, my dear friend, you shall be satisfied," returned he; "I believe the rain is not far off, and we shall soon see the first clouds in the south-west."

Banks was right. Towards evening the western horizon became obscured by vapours, showing that the monsoon, as frequently happens, would commence during the night. These mists, charged with electricity, came across the peninsula from the Indian Ocean, like so many vast leathern bottles out of the cellars of Æolus, filled full of storm, tempest, and hurricane.

Other signs, well-known to Anglo-Indians, were observed during the day. Spiral columns of very fine dust whirled along the roads, in a manner quite unlike that which was raised by our heavy wheels. They resembled a number of those tufts of downy wool which can be set in motion by an electrical machine. The ground might, therefore, be compared to an immense receiver in which for several days electricity had been stored up. This dust was strangely tinted with yellow, and had a most curious effect, each atom seeming to shine from a little luminous centre. At times we appeared to be travelling through flames, harmless flames, it is true, though neither in colour nor vivacity resembling the *ignis fatuus*.

Storr told us that he had sometimes seen trains pass along the rails between a double hedge of this luminous dust, and his statement was confirmed by Banks. During a quarter of an hour I watched very carefully this singular phenomenon from the windows of the turret on the engine, whence I could look along the route we were following for a considerable distance. There were no trees by the road, which was thickly covered with dust, intensely heated by the vertical rays of the sun. The burning heat of the atmosphere appeared to me just then to surpass that of our furnaces. It was insupportable, and, almost suffocated, I withdrew to breathe fresher air beneath the fanning wings of the punkah.

At about seven o'clock in the evening our train came to a halt. The place chosen by Banks was on the borders of a forest of magnificent banyans whose shade appeared to stretch northward to an infinite distance. A good road passed through this forest, and we promised ourselves a pleasanter journey next day beneath these wide and lofty domes of verdure.

The banyans, those giants of the Indian forest, stand surrounded by their children and grandchildren like patriarchs of the vegetable world. The young trees, springing from one common root, rise up around the main trunk, but completely detached from it, and mingle their branches with the towering verdure of the paternal stem. They give one the idea of having been hatched under this dense foliage, like chickens beneath their mother's wings. Hence the singular aspect of these venerable forests which have for age after age continued in this way to extend their limits. The old banyans resemble isolated pillars supporting an enormous vault, the finer arches and mouldings of which rest on the younger trees, they in their turn becoming main pillars.

On this evening the encampment was arranged with greater care than usual, because if the heat of the following day should prove equally overpowering, Banks proposed to prolong the halt, so as to pursue the journey during the night.

Colonel Munro was well pleased to think of spending some hours in this noble forest, so shady, so deeply calm. Everybody was satisfied with the arrangement; some because they really required rest, others because they longed once more to endeavour to fall in with some animal worth firing at. It is easy to guess who those persons were.

"Fox! Goûmi! it is only seven o'clock!" cried Captain Hood as soon as we came to a halt; "let's take a turn in the forest before it is quite dark. Will you come with us, Maucler?"

"My dear Hood," said Banks, before I had time to answer, "you had better not leave the encampment. The weather looks threatening. Should the storm burst, you would find some trouble in getting back to us. To-morrow if we remain here, you can go."

"But to-morrow it will be daylight again," replied Hood. "The dark hours are what I want for adventure!"

"I know that, Hood, but the night which is coming on is very unpromising. Still, if you are resolved to go, do not wander to any distance. In an hour, it will be very dark, and you might have great difficulty in making your way back to camp."

"Don't be uneasy, Banks; it is hardly seven o'clock, and I will only ask the colonel for leave of absence till ten."

"Go, if you wish it, my dear Hood," said Sir Edward "but pray attend to the advice Banks has given you."

"All right, colonel."

And the captain, with his followers Fox and Goûmi, all well equipped for the chase, left the encampment, and quickly disappeared behind the thick trees.

Fatigued by the heat of the day, I remained in camp.

Banks gave orders that the engine fires should not, as they usually were, be completely extinguished. He wished to retain the power of quickly getting up steam in case of an emergency.

Storr and Kâlouth betook themselves to their accustomed tasks, and attended to the supplies of wood and water; in doing so, they found little difficulty, for a small stream flowed near our halting-place, and there was no lack of timber close at hand. M. Parazard diligently laboured in his vocation, and, while putting aside the remains of one dinner, was busily planning the next.

As the evening continued pleasant, Sir Edward, Banks, McNeil, and I, went to rest by the borders of the rivulet, as the flow of its limpid waters refreshed the atmosphere, which even at this hour was suffocating.

The sinking sun shed a light which tinged with a colour like dark blue ink a mass of vapour which through openings in the dense foliage we could see accumulating in the zenith. These thick, heavily condensed clouds were stirred by no wind, but appeared to advance with a solemn motion of their own.

We remained chatting here till about eight o'clock. From time to time, Banks rose to take a more extended view of the horizon, going towards the borders of the forest which abruptly crossed the plain within a quarter of a mile of the camp. Each time on returning he looked uneasy, and only shook his head in reply to our questions.

At last we rose and accompanied him. Beneath the

banyans it began to be dark already; I could see that an immense plain stretched westward up to a line of indistinct low hills which were now almost enveloped in the clouds. The aspect of the heavens was terrible in its calm. Not a breath of air stirred the leaves of the highest trees. It was not the soft repose of slumbering nature so often sung by poets, but the dull heavy sleep of sickness. There was a restrained tension in the atmosphere, like condensed steam ready to explode.

And indeed the explosion was imminent. The storm clouds were high, as is usually the case over plains, and presented wide curvilinear outlines very strongly marked. They seemed to swell out, and, uniting together, diminished in number while they increased in size. Evidently, in a short time, there would be but one dense mass spread over the sky above us. Small detached clouds at a lower elevation hurried along, attracting, repelling, and crushing one against another, then, confusedly joining the general *mêlée*, were lost to view.

About half-past eight a sharp flash of forked lightning rent the gloom asunder.

Sixty-five seconds afterwards, a peal of thunder broke, and the hollow rumbling attendant to that species of lightning lasted about fifteen seconds.

"Sixteen miles," said Banks, looking at his watch. "That is almost the greatest distance at which thunder can be heard. But the storm, once unchained, will travel quickly; we must not wait for it. Let us go indoors, my friends."

"And what about Captain Hood?" said Sergeant McNeil.

"The thunder has sounded the recall," replied Banks. "It is to be hoped he will obey orders."

Five minutes afterwards we were seated under the verandah of our saloon.

CHAPTER XII.

THREE-FOLD LIGHT.

HINDOOSTAN shares with certain parts of Brazil—among others with Rio Janeiro—the proud distinction of being more frequently visited by storms than any other country on the face of the globe.

In France, England, Germany, and all the central parts of Europe, the average number of days on which thunder is heard is twenty per annum, while in the East Indies the average during the same time is more than fifty. That is the ordinary meteorological calculation.

On this particular occasion we had every reason, on account of various attendant circumstances, to expect a storm of extreme violence.

I consulted the barometer as soon as we re-entered our apartments, and found that there had been a sudden fall of two inches in the mercurial column.

This I pointed out to Colonel Munro.

"I am uneasy about Hood and his companions," he

said. "A storm is imminent; night is coming on, and the darkness rapidly increases. Sportsmen are certain always to go farther than they say they will, and even than they intend. How are they to find their way back to us?"

"Madman that he is!" cried Banks; "it was impossible to make him listen to reason. They never ought to have gone!"

"That is true enough, Banks; but gone they are," replied Sir Edward; "all we can do now is to try and get them back."

"Can we signal to them, anyhow?" I asked.

"To be sure we can. I will light the electric lamps at once. That is a happy thought of yours, Maucler."

"Shall I go in search of Captain Hood, sir?" inquired McNeil.

"No, my old friend," replied the colonel. "You would not find him, and would be lost yourself."

Banks connected the electric current, and very soon Behemoth's eyes, like two blazing beacons, shot glaring light athwart the gloom of the banyan forest. It seemed certain that it would be visible to our sportsmen at a considerable distance.

At this moment a hurricane of great violence burst forth, rending the tree-tops, and sounding among the columns of banyan as though rushing through sonorous organ-pipes.

It was indeed a sudden outburst. Showers of leaves and dead branches strewed the ground, and rattled upon the roofs of our carriages.

We closed every window; but the rain did not yet fall.

"It is a species of typhoon," remarked Banks.

The Hindoos give this name to the sudden and impetuous tempests which devastate more especially the mountainous districts, and are much dreaded by the natives.

"Storr!" cried Banks to the engine-driver, "are the embrasures of the turret well closed?"

"Yes, Mr. Banks; there is nothing to fear there."

"Where is Kâlouth?"

"He is stowing away the last of the fuel in the tender."

"After this storm we shall only have to collect the wood. The wind is playing wood-cutter, and sparing us all the hard work," said the engineer. "Keep up the pressure, Storr, and get under shelter."

"Ay, ay, sir."

"Are your tanks filled, Kâlouth?"

"Yes, sahib; the water supply is made up."

"Well, come in, come in."

And the engine-driver and stoker hastened into the second carriage.

Flashes of lightning were now frequent, and thunder from the electric clouds kept up a sullen roar. The wind blew like scorching blasts from the mouth of a furnace. Occasionally we left the saloon, and went into the verandah. Gazing upward at the lofty summits of the stately banyans, the branches showed like fine black lace against the glowing background of the illumined sky. The incessant lightning was followed so rapidly by the peals of thunder, that the echoes had not time to die away; they were continually aroused by new and yet louder explosions. A deep, continuous roll was maintained, and only broken by those sharp detonations so well compared by Lucretius to the harsh screaming sound of paper when it is torn.

"I wonder the storm has not yet driven them in," said Colonel Munro.

"Perhaps Captain Hood has found some shelter in the forest," answered Sergeant McNeil. "He may be waiting in some cave or hollow tree, and will rejoin us in the morning. The camp will be here all right."

Banks shook his head somewhat doubtfully; he did not seem to share McNeil's opinion.

It was now about nine o'clock; and the rain began to fall with great force. It was mingled with enormous hailstones, and they pelted on the hollow roofs of Steam House with a noise like the roll of many drums. Even without the roar of the thunder, it was impossible to hear our own voices. The air was full of the leaves of trees, whirling in all directions.

Banks did not attempt to speak, but pointed to the engine, directing our attention to the hailstones as they struck the metal sides of Behemoth. It was marvellous! Each stone struck fire in the contact, like flint and steel. It seemed as though showers of fiery metallic drops fell from the clouds, sending forth sparks as they struck the steel-plated engine. This proved how completely the atmosphere was saturated with electricity. Fulminating matter traversed it incessantly, till all space seemed to blaze with fire.

Banks signed to us to return to the saloon, and closed the verandah door. The darkness within the room contrasted strongly with the lightning which flashed without. We had presently a proof that we were ourselves strongly charged with the electric fluid, when, to our infinite astonishment, we perceived our saliva to be luminous. This phenomenon, rarely observed, and very alarming when it is so, has been described as " spitting fire."

The tumult of the heavens seemed every instant to increase, and the stoutest hearts beat thick and fast.

" And the others!" said Colonel Munro.

" Ah, yes, indeed—the others!" returned Banks.

We were horribly uneasy, yet could do nothing whatever to assist Captain Hood and his companions, who were of course in the utmost danger.

Even supposing they had found shelter, it could only be

beneath trees, where accidents during storms are most imminent, and in the middle of a dense forest, how could they possibly maintain the distance of five or six yards from a vertical line drawn from the extremity of the longest branches, which persons caught by storms in the neighbourhood of trees are scientifically advised to do.

As these thoughts rushed through my mind, a peal of thunder, louder than any we had heard, burst directly over us.

Steam House trembled throughout, and seemed to rise on its springs. I expected it to be overturned.

At the same time a strong odour filled the room—the penetrating smell of nitrous vapours.

"A thunder-bolt has fallen!" said McNeil.

"Storr! Kâlouth! Parazard!" shouted Banks.

The three men came running into our apartment, while the engineer stepped out on the balcony.

"There!—Look there!" he cried.

An enormous banyan had been struck ten paces off, on the left of the road.

We could see everything distinctly by the glare of incessant lightning. The immense trunk had fallen across the neighbouring trees, its sturdy saplings no longer able to sustain it. The whole length of its bark had been peeled off, and one long strip was waving about and lashing the air, as the force of the gale made it twist and twine like a serpent. It was seen that the bark must have been stripped off from base to summit, under the influence of electricity which had violently rushed upwards.

"A narrow escape for Steam House," said the engineer. "We must remain here; we are safer than under those trees.

As he spoke, we heard cries. Could it be our friends returning?

"It is Parazard's voice," said Storr.

It was indeed the cook, who, from the hinder balcony, was loudly calling to us. We hastened to join him.

What a sight met our eyes! Within a hundred yards of us, behind, and to the right of, the camp, the banyan forest was on fire!

Already the loftier tree-tops were disappearing behind a curtain of flame.

The conflagration advanced fiercely, and with incredible velocity towards Steam House. The danger was imminent. The heat and long continuous drought had combined to to make trees, grass, and bushes so dry and combustible that it was probable the entire forest would be devoured by the furious element.

As we witnessed its rapid spread and advance, we were convinced that should it reach the place of our encampment, our entire equipage would, in a very few minutes, be destroyed.

We stood silent before this fearful danger.

Then, folding his arms, the colonel said quietly,—

"Banks, you must get us out of this scrape!"

"Yes, I must, Munro," replied the engineer, "and since we cannot possibly put out this fire, we must run away from it."

"On foot?" exclaimed I.

"No; with our train all complete."

"And Captain Hood, sir?" said McNeil.

"We can do nothing for them. If they are not here immediately, we shall start without them."

"We must not abandon them," said the colonel.

"My dear Munro, let me get the train out of reach of the fire, and then we can search for them."

"Go on, then, Banks," replied Colonel Munro, who saw that the engineer was in the right.

"Storr!" cried Banks, "to your engine at once! Kâlouth! to your furnace—get the steam up! What pressure have we?"

"Two atmospheres," answered the engine-driver.

"Within ten minutes we must have four! Look sharp, my lads!"

The men did not lose a moment.

Torrents of black smoke gushed from the elephant's trunk, meeting, and seeming to defy, the torrents of rain. Behemoth replied with whirling clouds of sparks to the vivid flashes which surrounded him; and draughts of air, whistling through the funnel, accelerated the combustion of the wood, which Kâlouth heaped and piled on his furnace.

Sir Edward Munro, Banks, and I, remained on the verandah in rear of the carriages, watching the progress of the forest fire. Huge trees tottered and fell across this vast hearth, the branches cracked and crackled like musketry, the burning creepers twisted in all directions, and led the flames from tree to tree, thus spreading the devastation right and left.

Within five minutes, the conflagration had advanced fifty yards, and the flames, torn and dishevelled by the gale, shot upward to such a height that the lightning flashes pierced them in all directions.

"We must be off in five minutes," said Banks.

"At what a pace this fire goes!" I replied.

"We shall go faster!"

"If only Hood and his men were back!" said Sir Edward.

"The whistle!—sound the whistle!" cried Banks, "they may, perhaps, hear that."

And darting into the turret, he made the air resound with shrill screams, which were heard above the rumbling thunder, and must have sounded to an immense distance.

The situation can better be imagined than described.

Necessity urged to immediate flight, while it seemed impossible to forsake our absent friends.

Banks returned to the hinder balcony. The edge of the fire was less than fifty yards from Steam House. The heat became insufferable, we could scarcely breathe the burning air. Flakes of fire fell on the carriages, which seemed protected in a measure by the floods and torrents of rain, but these, we well knew, could not check the direct attack of the flames.

The engine continued to send forth piercing shrieks. It was all in vain. There were no signs of either Hood, Fox, or Goumi.

The engine-driver came to Banks,—

"Steam is up, sir!" said he.

"Go on, then, Storr!" replied Banks, "but not too fast. Just quick enough to keep us beyond the reach of the fire."

"Stop, Banks! wait a few minutes!" cried Colonel Munro, who could not bring himself to quit the spot.

"Three minutes, then, Munro," returned Banks coolly. "But in three minutes the back of the train will begin to burn."

Two minutes passed. It was impossible to stay in the verandah. The iron plating could not be touched, and began to burst open at the joints. It would be madness to stop another instant.

"Go on, Storr!"

"Hallo!" exclaimed the sergeant.

"There they are! God be praised!" said the colonel.

To the right of the road appeared Captain Hood and Fox, supporting Goûmi in their arms as they approached the carriage-door.

"Is he dead?"

"No; but struck by lightning, which smashed his gun, and has paralyzed his left leg."

"We should never have got back to camp but for your steam whistle, Banks!" said Hood.

"Forward! forward!" shouted the engineer.

Hood and Fox sprang on board the train, and Goûmi, who had not lost consciousness, was placed in his cabin.

It was half-past ten—Banks and Storr went into the turret, and the equipage moved steadily forward, amid the blaze of a three-fold light, produced by the burning forest, the electric lamps, and the vivid lightning flashing from the skies.

Then Captain Hood in a few words related what had happened during his excursion. They had seen no traces of any wild animals. As the storm approached, darkness overtook them much more rapidly than they expected. They were three miles from camp when they heard the first thunder-clap, and endeavoured to return, but quickly found they had lost their way among the banyan trunks, all exactly alike, and without a path in any direction whatever.

The tempest increased in violence, they were far beyond the limits of the light diffused by our electric lamp, and had nothing to guide them as to our whereabouts, while the rain and hail fell in torrents, quickly penetrating the shelter of the leafy screen above them.

Suddenly with a glare of intensely brilliant lightning a burst of thunder broke over them, and Goûmi fell prostrate at Captain Hood's feet; the butt-end of his gun alone remained in his hand, for it was instantaneously stripped of every bit of metal. They believed him to be killed, but found that the electric fluid had not struck him directly, although his leg was paralyzed by the shock. Poor Goûmi could not walk a step, and had to be carried. His companions would not listen to his entreaties that they would leave him, escape themselves, and if possible return afterwards to fetch him. They raised him between them, and, as best they could, pursued their doubtful way through the dark forest.

Thus for two hours they wandered about, hesitating, stopping, resuming their march, without the slightest clue to the direction in which to find the camp.

At last, to their infinite joy, they heard the shriek of the steam whistle. It was the welcome voice of Behemoth.

A quarter of an hour afterwards they arrived as we were

on the point of quitting the halting-place, and only just in time!

And now though the train ran rapidly along the broad, smooth forest road, the fire kept pace with it, and the danger was rendered the more threatening by a change of wind, such as frequently occurs during these violent meteoric storms. Instead of blowing in flank, it now changed to the rear, and by its vehemence materially increased the advance of the flames which perceptibly gained on the travellers. A cloud of hot ashes whirled upwards from the ground, as from the mouth of some crater; and into this rained downwards burning branches and flakes of fire. The conflagration really resembled more than anything else the advance of a stream of lava, rushing across the country, and destroying everything in its course

Banks instantly perceived this, and even if he had not, he would have felt the scorching blast as it swept by.

Our speed was increased, although some danger attended the doing so over an unknown path. The machine, however, would not proceed as fast as the engineer could have wished, owing to the road being so cut up and flooded by rain.

About half-past eleven, another awful clap of thunder burst directly over our heads. A cry escaped us. We feared that Banks and Storr had both been struck in their howdah, from which they were guiding the train.

This calamity, however, had not befallen us. Our elephant only had been struck, the tip of one of his long hanging ears having attracted the electric current. No damage resulted to the machine fortunately, and Behemoth seemed to try to reply to the peals of thunder by renewed and vigorous trumpetings.

"Hurrah!" cried Captain Hood. "Hurrah! An elephant of flesh and blood would have been done for by this time. But this old fellow braves thunder and lightning, and sticks at nothing. Go it, Behemoth; hurrah!"

For another half-hour the train was still ahead. Banks, fearing to run it against some obstacle, only proceeded at a rate sufficient to keep us out of reach of the fire.

From the verandah, in which Colonel Munro, Hood, and I had placed ourselves, we could see passing, great shadows, bounding through the blaze of the fire and lightning. We soon discovered them to be those of wild animals.

As a precautionary measure, Captain Hood kept his gun ready, for it was possible that some terrified beast might leap on our train, in search of a shelter or refuge.

One huge tiger did indeed make the attempt, but in his prodigious spring, he was caught by the neck between two branches of a banyan-tree, which, bending under the storm, acted like great cords, and strangled the animal.

"Poor beast!" said Fox.

"These creatures," remarked Captain Hood, in an indignant manner, "are made to be killed by good, honest shot. You may well say poor beast."

Poor Captain Hood was indeed out of luck. When he wanted tigers, he couldn't find them, and now when he was not looking for them, they passed within range, without his being able to get a shot at them, or were strangled before his eyes like mice in a trap.

At one in the morning, our situation, dangerous as it had been before, became worse. The wind, which shifted about from one point of the compass to another, continually swept the fire across the road in front of us, so that now we were absolutely hemmed in.

The storm, however, had much diminished in violence, as is invariably the case when these meteors pass above a forest, for there the trees gradually draw off, and absorb the electric matter. But though the lightning and thunder were now less frequent, and though the rain fell with gentler force, yet the wind still roared with inconceivable fury.

At any cost it was absolutely necessary to hasten on, even at the risk of running into an obstacle, or of dashing over a precipice.

Banks directed our course with astonishing coolness, his eyes glued to the glass of the howdah, his hand ever on the regulator.

Our way now led between two hedges of fire, and these we were forced to go through. On went Banks, resolutely and steadily at the rate of five or six miles an hour.

I thought at last we should be obliged to stop when before us lay a narrow passage, only fifty yards wide, with a roaring furnace on either side. Our wheels crunched over the glowing cinders which strewed the soil, and a burning, stifling atmosphere enveloped us.

We were past !

At two in the morning a flash of lightning revealed to us the borders of the wood. Behind us lay a vast panorama of flames, which would spread on, and never stop until they had devoured the very last banyan of the immense forest.

At daybreak we halted at last; the storm had entirely ceased, and we arranged our camp.

Our elephant, who was carefully examined, was found to have the tip of his right ear pierced by several holes running in diverse directions. If such a thing had happened to any other creature than an animal of steel, it would most certainly have at once sunk down, never again to rise, and our unfortunate train would then have been rapidly overwhelmed by the advancing flames.

At six that morning, after a very short rest, we again resumed our journey, and by twelve o'clock we were encamped in the neighbourhood of Rewah.

CHAPTER XIII.

CAPTAIN HOOD'S PROWESS.

THE remainder of the day and the next night were quietly spent in camp. After all our fatigue and danger, this rest was well earned.

We had no longer before us the rich plains of the kingdom of Oude. Steam House had now to pass through Rohilkund, a fertile territory, though much cut up by "nullahs," or ravines. Bareilly is the capital of this province, which is 155 miles square, well watered by the numerous affluents or tributaries of the Cogra; here and there are many groups of magnificent mango-trees, as well as thick jungles, which latter are gradually disappearing as cultivation advances.

After the taking of Delhi, this was the centre of the insurrection; Sir Colin Campbell conducted one of his campaigns here. Here, too, Brigadier Walpole's column was not at the outset very fortunate, and here also, fell a friend of Sir Edward Munro, the colonel of the 93rd Highlanders, who had so distinguished himself in the two assaults on Lucknow, during the affair of the 14th of April.

We could not have had a country better suited for the advance of our train than this. Beautiful level roads, easily crossed streams, running from the two more importaat arteries, descending from the north, all united to render this part of our journey pleasant. In a short time we should come to the first rising ground which connected the plain with the mountains of Nepaul.

We had, however, to think seriously of the rainy season.

The monsoon, which is prevalent from the north-east to the south-west during the first months of the year, is now reversed. The rainy season is more violent on the coast than in the interior of the peninsula, and also a little later; the reason being that the clouds are exhausted before reaching the centre of India. Besides this, their direction is somewhat altered by the barrier of high mountains which form a sort of atmospheric eddy. On the coast of Malabar the monsoon begins in the month of May; in the central and northern provinces, it is felt some weeks later on, in June. We were now in June, and our journey was henceforward to be performed under new though well foreseen circumstances.

I should have said before that honest Goûmi, who had been disarmed by the lightning in such an untoward manner, was nearly well again by the next day. The paralysis of his left leg was merely temporary. Soon not a trace of his accident remained, but it seemed to me he always bore rather a grudge against that storm.

On both the 6th and 7th of June, Captain Hood, aided by Fan and Niger, had better sport. He killed a couple of those antelopes called "nylghaus." They are the blue oxen of the Hindoos, though it is certainly more correct to call them deer, since they have a greater resemblance to that animal than to the congeners of the god Apis. They may better be described as pearl-grey deer, for their colour is more like a stormy than an azure sky. It is, however, asserted that some of these magnificent creatures, with little sharp, straight horns on their long, slightly convex heads, have really almost blue coats—a tint which Nature appears to have invariably refused to quadrupeds, even to the blue fox, whose fur is rather black than blue.

These were not the wild beasts Captain Hood hoped for; but all the same, the nylghau, though not actually ferocious, is dangerous; for when slightly wounded, it turns on the hunter.

A shot from the captain, and a second from Fox, stopped short both of these superb creatures, killed, as it were, on the wing; and indeed Fox seemed to look on them as nothing higher than feathered game.

Monsieur Parazard, fortunately, was quite of another opinion, and the excellent haunch, cooked to a turn, which he served up to us that day at dinner, brought us all over to his side.

At daybreak on the 8th of June we left an encampment we had made near a little village in Rohilkund. We had arrived at it the evening before, after traversing the twenty-five miles which lay between it and Rewah. Our train could only go at a very moderate pace over the heavy ground caused by the rains. Besides this, the streams began to swell, and fording several delayed us some hours. After all we had not now so very far to go. We were sure of reaching the mountainous region before the end of June. There we intended to instal Steam House for several of the summer months, as if in the midst of a sanitorium. We had nothing to make us uneasy in that respect.

On the 8th of June Captain Hood missed a fine opportunity for a shot.

The road was bordered by a thick bamboo jungle, as is often the case near villages, which look as if built in a basket of flowers. This was not as yet the true jungle, for that, in the Hindoo sense, applies to the rugged, bare, and sterile plain, dotted with lines of grey bushes. We, on the contrary, were in a cultivated country, in the midst of a fertile territory, covered in most places with marshy rice-grounds.

Behemoth went quietly along, guided by Storr's hand,

and emitting graceful, feathery clouds of vapour, which curled away and dispersed among the bamboos at the roadside.

All at once, out leapt an animal with the most wonderful agility, and fastened on our elephant's neck.

"A cheetah! a cheetah!" shouted the engine-driver.

At this cry, Captain Hood darted out to the balcony, and seized his gun, always ready and always at hand.

"A cheetah!" exclaimed he in his turn.

"Fire, then!" cried I.

"Time enough!" returned the captain, who contented himself with merely taking a good aim at the animal.

The cheetah is a species of leopard peculiar to India, not so large as the tiger, but almost as formidable, it is so active, supple, and strong.

Colonel Munro, Banks, and I stood out on the verandah, watching with interest for the captain to fire.

The leopard had evidently been deceived by the sight of our elephant. He had boldly sprung at him, expecting to bury his teeth and claws in living flesh, but instead of that, met with an iron skin, on which neither teeth nor claws could make any impression. Furious at his discomfiture, he clung to the long ears of the artificial animal, and was no doubt preparing to bound off again when he caught sight of us.

Captain Hood kept his gun pointed after the manner of

a hunter who is sure of his aim, but does not wish to fire until he is certain he can hit a vital part.

The cheetah drew itself up, roaring savagely. It no doubt knew of its danger, but did not attempt to escape. Perhaps it watched for an opportunity to spring on to the verandah.

Indeed, we soon saw it climbing up the elephant's head, to the trunk or chimney, and almost to the opening, out of which puffed jets of vapour.

"Now fire, Hood!" said I again.

"There's time enough," answered the captain.

Then, without taking his eyes off the leopard, who still gazed at us, he addressed himself to me.

"Did you ever kill a cheetah, Maucler?" he asked.

"Never."

"Would you like to kill one?"

"Captain," I replied, "I should not like to deprive you of this magnificent shot—"

"Pooh!" returned Hood, "it's nothing of a shot. Take a gun and aim just below the beast's shoulder! If you miss, I shall catch him as he springs."

"Be it so, then."

Fox, who had joined us, put a double-barrelled gun into my hands. I took it, cocked it, aimed just below the leopard's shoulder, and fired.

The animal, wounded, though but slightly, took an enormous bound, right over the driver's howdah, and alighted on the first roof of Steam House.

Skilled sportsman as Captain Hood was, even he had not time to fire.

"Here, Fox, after me!" he shouted.

And the two, darting out of the verandah, hastened up into the howdah.

The leopard immediately sprang on to the second roof, clearing the foot-bridge at a bound.

The captain was on the point of firing, but another desperate leap carried the animal off the roof, and landed him at the side of the road, when he instantly disappeared in the jungle.

"Stop! stop!" cried Banks, to the engineer, who, applying the atmospheric brakes, brought the train to an instant standstill.

The captain and Fox leapt out and ran into the thicket, in hopes of finding the cheetah.

A few minutes passed. We listened somewhat impatiently. No shot was fired, and very soon the two hunters returned empty handed.

"Disappeared! Got clear off!" called out Captain Hood; "and not even a trace of blood on the grass!"

"It was my fault," said I. "It would have been better if you had fired at the cheetah yourself. You wouldn't have missed!"

"Nonsense," returned Hood, "you hit him, I'm certain, though not in a good place."

"The beast wasn't fated to be my thirty-ninth, nor your forty-first, captain," remarked Fox, much out of countenance.

"Rubbish," said Hood, in a somewhat affected tone of indifference, "a cheetah isn't a tiger! If it had been, my dear Maucler, I couldn't have made up my mind to yield that shot to you!"

"Come to table, my friends," said Colonel Munro. "Breakfast is ready and will console you—"

"I hope it may," put in McNeil; "but it was all Fox's fault!"

"My fault?" said the man, quite nonplussed by this unexpected observation.

"Certainly, Fox," returned the sergeant. "The gun you handed to Mr. Maucler was only loaded with number six!"

And McNeil held out the second cartridge which he had just withdrawn, to prove his words.

"Fox!" said Captain Hood.

"Yes, sir."

"A couple of days under arrest!"

"Yes, captain."

And Fox retired into his cabin, resolved not to appear again for forty-eight hours.

He was quite ashamed of himself, and wished to hide his disgraced head.

The next day Captain Hood, Goûmi, and I went off to beat about the plain at the side of the road, and thus to spend the half-day's halt which Banks allowed us. It rained all the morning, but about midday the sky cleared, and we hoped for a few hours of fine weather.

I must mention that it was not Hood, the hunter of wild beasts, who took me out this time, but the sportsman in search of game. In the interests of the table, he intended to stroll quietly about the rice-fields, accompanied by Fan and Niger.

Monsieur Parazard had hinted to the captain that his larder was empty, and that he expected his honour to take the necessary measures to fill it again.

Captain Hood resigned himself, and we set out. For two hours our battue had no other result than to put up a few partridges, or scare away a few hares; but all at such a distance that, notwithstanding our good dogs, we had no chance of hitting them.

Captain Hood became utterly disgusted. In this vast plain, without jungles, or thickets, and dotted with villages and farms, he had no great hopes of meeting with any sort of wild beast, which would make amends for the loss of the leopard the preceding day. He had only come out now in the character of a purveyor, and thought of the reception

Monsieur Parazard would give him if he returned with an empty bag.

It was not our fault that even by four o'clock we had not had occasion to fire a single shot. A dry wind blew, and, as I said, all the game rose out of range.

"My dear fellow," said Hood, "this won't do at all. When we left Calcutta, I promised you such grand sport; and all this time, bad luck, fatality, I don't know what to call it, nor how to understand it, has prevented me from keeping my promise!"

"Come, captain," I replied, "you musn't despair. Though I do regret it, it is more on your account than my own! We shall have better luck, no doubt, on the hills!"

"Yes," said Hood, "on the Himalayan slopes, we shall set to work under more favourable conditions. You see, Maucler, I'd wager anything that our train, with all its apparatus, its steam and its roaring, and especially the gigantic elephant, terrifies the confounded brutes much more than a railway train would do, and that's the reason we don't see anything of them when travelling! When we halt, we must hope to be more lucky. That leopard was a fool! He must have been starving when he sprang on Behemoth, and he was worthy of being killed outright by a good shot! Hang that fellow Fox! I shan't forget that little job of his in a hurry! What time is it now?"

"Nearly five o'clock!"

"Five already, and we haven't bagged a thing!"

"They won't expect us back in camp till seven. Perhaps by that time—"

"No; luck is against us!" exclaimed the captain; "and look you, luck is the half of success!"

"Perseverance too," I answered. "Suppose we agree that we won't go back empty-handed! Will that suit you?"

"Suit me? of course it will!"

"Agreed, then."

"Look here, Maucler, I shall carry back a mouse or a squirrel rather than be foresworn."

Hood, Goûmi, and I, were now in a frame of mind to attack anything. The chase was continued with a perseverance worthy of a better cause; but it seemed as if even the most inoffensive birds had become aware of our hostile intentions. We couldn't get near a single one.

We roamed about thus among the rice-fields, beating first one side of the road and then the other, and turning back again, so as not to get too far from the camp. All was useless. Half-past six, and we had not had to reload our guns. We might as well have had walking-sticks in our hands, the results would have been all the same.

I glanced at Captain Hood. He was marching along with his teeth set, while a deep frown on his brow betrayed his angry feelings. Between his compressed lips he muttered I don't know what vain menaces against every living creature whether feathered or furred of which there was not a specimen on the plain. He probably would soon fire his gun at the first object which met his eye, a tree or rock maybe—rather a cynical way of getting rid of his anger. It was easy to see his weapon burned his fingers, as it were, from the way he shifted it about, now to his shoulder, then to his arm, now again carrying it in his hand.

Goûmi looked at him.

"The captain will be in a passion if this goes on!" he said to me, shaking his head.

"Yes," I replied, "I'd willingly give thirty shillings for the most modest little tame pigeon, if some charitable hand would let it go within range! It would appease him!"

But neither for thirty shillings, nor for double, or triple that amount, could we procure even the cheapest or the most common of fowl. The country seemed deserted, and we saw neither farm nor village.

Indeed if it had been possible, I believe I should have sent Goûmi to buy at any price some bird or other, if only a plucked chicken, anything to set our fretful captain free from his vow.

Night was coming on. In an hour's time there would

not be light enough for us to continue our fruitless expedition. Although we had agreed not to return to camp without something, yet we should be forced to do so, unless we meant to stay out all night. Not only did it threaten rain, but Colonel Munro and Banks would be seriously alarmed if we did not reappear.

Captain Hood, with straining eyeballs, glancing from right to left with bird-like quickness, walked ten paces ahead in an opposite direction to that of "Steam House."

I was thinking of hastening my steps so as to rejoin him and beg him not to continue this struggle against ill-luck, when a whirr of wings was heard on my right. I looked towards the spot.

A dark mass was rising slowly above a thicket.

Instantly, without giving Captain Hood time to turn round, I levelled my gun, and fired both barrels successively. The unknown bird fell heavily.

Fan sprang forward, seized and brought it to the captain.

"At last!" exclaimed Hood. "If Monsieur Parazard isn't contented with this, he must be shoved into his pot himself, head first."

"But is it an edible bird?" I asked.

"Certainly, for want of anything better!" answered the captain.

"It was lucky nobody saw you, Mr. Maucler!" said Goûmi.

"What have I done wrong?"

"Why, you have killed a peacock, and that is forbidden, for they are sacred birds all over India."

"The fiend fly away with sacred birds and those who made them sacred too!" exclaimed Captain Hood impatiently. "This one is killed at all events, and we shall eat him—devoutly if you like, but devour him somehow!"

Since the expedition of Alexander into this peninsula, the peacock has been a sacred animal in the Brahmins' country. The Hindoos make it the emblem of the goddess Saravasti, who presides over births and marriages. To destroy this bird is forbidden under pain of punishment, which the English law has confirmed.

This one, which so rejoiced Captain Hood's heart was a magnificent specimen, with green metallic gleaming wings, edged with gold. His beautifully marked tail formed a superb fan of silky feathers.

"All right, forward!" said the captain.

"To-morrow, Monsieur Parazard will give us peacock for dinner, in spite of what all the Brahmins in India may think! Although, when cooked, this bird will indeed only look like a somewhat pretentious chicken, yet with its feathers artistically arranged, it will have a fine effect on our table!"

"Then you are satisfied, captain?"

"Satisfied—with you, yes, my dear fellow, but not pleased

with myself at all! My bad luck isn't over yet, and I must do away with it. Come along!"

Off we started to retrace our steps to the camp, now about three miles distant. Captain Hood and I walked close together along a winding path through thick bamboo jungles; Goûmi, carrying our game, bringing up the rear. The sun had not yet disappeared, but it was shrouded in great clouds, so that we had to find our way through semi-obscurity.

All at once a terrific roar burst from a thicket on our right. The sound was to me so awful that I stopped short, almost in spite of myself.

Captain Hood grasped my hand.

"A tiger!" he said.

Then an oath escaped him.

"Thunder and lightning!" he exclaimed, "there is only small shot in our guns!"

It was too true, neither Hood, Goumi, nor I, had any ball cartridges!

Besides, if we had, we should not have had time to reload. Ten seconds after uttering his first roar, the animal leapt from the covert with a single bound, and landed on the road twenty paces from us.

It was a magnificent tiger, what the Hindoos would have called a man-eater, his annual victims might no doubt be counted by hundreds.

CAPTAIN HOOD'S PROWESS.

The situation was terrible.

I gazed at the tiger, and must confess that my gun trembled in my hand. He measured from nine to ten feet in length, and was of a tawny colour, striped with black and white.

He stared back at us, his cat-like eyes blazing in the shadow. His tail feverishly lashed his sides. He crouched as if about to spring.

Hood had not lost his presence of mind. He took a careful aim at the animal, muttering in a tone which it is impossible to describe,—

"Number six! To fire at a tiger with number six! If I don't hit him right in the eyes, we are—"

The captain had not time to finish. The tiger advanced not by leaps, but slow steps.

Goûmi crouched behind us, and also took aim, though his gun too only contained small shot. As to mine, it was not even loaded. I prepared to do this now.

"Not a movement, not a sound!" muttered the captain. "The tiger will spring, and that will never do!"

We all three remained motionless.

The tiger advanced slowly, his eyes glaring fixedly, and his great jaws held almost level with the ground.

The brute was now only ten paces from the captain.

Hood stood firm, steady as a statue, concentrating his whole life in his gaze.

The terrible struggle which was about to take place, and which might leave none of us alive, did not even make his heart beat more rapidly than usual.

I thought the tiger was about to make his spring.

He took five steps. I had need of all my self-control to keep from calling out,—

"Fire, Hood! now fire!"

No! The captain had said—and it was evidently his only chance—that he meant to blind the animal; and to do that he must be very close before he fired.

The tiger came three paces nearer, and prepared to spring—

A loud report was heard, almost immediately followed by a second.

The second explosion seemed to have taken place in the very body of the animal, which after two or three starts and roars of pain, fell dead on the ground.

"Wonderful!" exclaimed Captain Hood, "my gun was loaded with ball after all, and what's more, with an explosive ball! Ah, thanks, Fox, this time, many thanks!"

"Is it possible?" I cried.

"Look for yourself."

And as he spoke the captain drew out the cartridge from the other barrel.

There was the ball.

All was explained.

Captain Hood possessed a double-barrelled rifle and a double-barrelled gun, both of the same calibre. Now, when Fox made the mistake of loading the rifle with small shot, he at the same time put explosive ball cartridges into the other. The day before, this mistake saved the life of the leopard, to-day it saved ours!

"Yes," remarked Hood, "and never in my life have I been nearer death!"

Half-an-hour afterwards, when we were safe back in camp, Hood called up Fox and told him what had happened.

"Captain," returned the man, "that proves that instead of two days in confinement, I deserved four, because I made a mistake twice!"

"That is my opinion," replied his master; "but since through your mistake I have bagged my forty-first, it is also my opinion that I should offer you this sovereign—"

"And mine, that I should take it," answered Fox, pocketing the piece of gold.

Such were the incidents which marked Captain Hood's encounter with his forty-first tiger.

In the evening of the 12th of June, our train came to a halt near a small village of no importance, and the next day we set out to begin the ninety miles which still lay between us and the mountains of Nepaul.

CHAPTER XIV.

ONE AGAINST THREE.

SOME days passed away, and we had at last commenced to ascend the first slopes of those northern regions of India, which from rising ground to rising grouud, from hill to hill, from mountain to mountain, at last attain to the highest altitude on the globe. Till then we had been rising, but so imperceptibly that Behemoth did not even appear to perceive it.

The weather was stormy and rainy, but the temperature was supportable. The roads were not yet bad, and heavy as the train was, it passed easily over them.

When too large a rut opened before us, Storr just touched the regulator, and a stronger press of the obedient fluid was enough to take us over the obstacle. The machine, as I said, had plenty of power, and a quarter of a turn, given to the supply valves, instantly added immensely to its strength.

As yet, we never had reason but to congratulate ourselves on this species of locomotion, as well as on the engine Banks had invented. Our rolling house was perfectly comfortable, and before our eyes we had always a fresh and ever-changing landscape.

The vast plain which extends from the valley of the Ganges into the territories of Oude and Rohilkund was ended. The north was framed in by the summits of the Himalayas, against which were swept the clouds driven by the south-west wind. It was impossible as yet to get a good view of the picturesque outline of this lofty chain; but on approaching the Thibetian frontier, the aspect of the country became more wild, and the jungle increased at the expense of cultivated ground.

The flora too, was no longer the same. Palms had disappeared, to give place to magnificent bananas, tufted mangoes bearing the best Indian fruit, and especially groups of bamboos, many shooting up to a hundred feet in height. Here we found magnolias, scenting the air with delicious perfume, from their large white blossoms; beautiful maples; various kinds of oaks; chestnuts, their fruit covered with prickles like sea-urchins; india-rubber trees, in which the sap flows through half-open veins; and pines with enormous leaves; then, more modest as to size, but gayer as to colour, were geraniums, rhododendrons, and laurels, thickly bordering the road.

A few villages composed of straw or bamboo-built huts,

two or three farms, buried among the great trees, were still to be met with, though many miles apart. As we approached higher ground, the population became less and less.

At that time a grey and misty sky hung over the whole landscape, and rain frequently fell in torrents. Out of four days, from the 13th to the 17th of June, we had not had it fine for six hours. We were obliged therefore to remain in the drawing-room of Steam House, and pass the long hours as we would if our dwelling had been a fixture, smoking, chatting, and playing whist.

For long our guns had been idle, to Captain Hood's great dissatisfaction; but two "slams," which he made in a single evening, brought him back to his accustomed goodhumour.

"One can kill a tiger any day," he remarked, "but one can't always make a slam!"

Such a correct and clear proposition was unanswerable.

On the 17th of June our camp was made near a serai— or traveller's bungalow. The weather was rather brighter, and Behemoth, who had been worked hard for the last four days, required, if not rest, at any rate some attention. It was therefore agreed that the rest of the day and the following night, should be passed in this spot.

The serai or caravanserai, the inn to be found on all the high roads, is a quadrangle of low buildings, surrounding an inner court, and usually surmounted by a tower at each corner, giving it quite an oriental appearance. The attendants in the serai consist of the "bhisti," or water-carrier, the cook, who does well enough for travellers who can content themselves with eggs and chickens, and the "khansama," or provider of provisions, with whom you must treat, and whose prices are low enough generally.

The keeper of the serai is simply an agent of the Honourable Company, to whom the greater number of these establishments belong, and they are inspected occasionally by the engineer-in-chief of the district.

A strange but strictly kept rule is in force in these bungalows: a traveller may occupy the serai for four-and-twenty hours, unquestioned, but in the event of his wishing to stay longer, he must get a permit from the inspector. Without this authorization the next comer, whether English or Hindoo, may turn him out.

It is needless to say that on our arrival at our halting-place, Behemoth produced the usual sensation, that is to say, he was very much stared at, and perhaps very much coveted. I must say, though, that the actual guests in the serai looked at him with somewhat of disdain, disdain too affected to be real.

These people, however, were not simple mortals, travelling on business or pleasure. It was not some English officer, on his way to the cantonments on the Nepaul frontier, not even a Hindoo merchant, leading his caravan to the Steppes of Afghanistan, beyond Lahore or Peshawar.

Here was nothing less than the Prince Gourou Singh, in person, son of an independent rajah of Guzarate, and a rajah himself, travelling with great pomp in the north of the Indian peninsula.

This prince not only occupied the three or four rooms in the bungalow, but also all the neighbourhood, which had been arranged so as to lodge the people of his suite.

I had never before seen a travelling rajah; so as soon as our camp had been settled at about a quarter of a mile from the serai, in a charming spot beside a stream and under magnificent trees, I went, in company with Captain Hood and Banks, to visit the encampment of Prince Gourou Singh.

The son of a rajah who wishes to travel, cannot travel alone, that is evident! If there are any people in the world whom I have not the slightest inclination to envy, they are those who can't move hand or foot, without putting in motion at least a hundred people! Far better to be the simplest pedestrian, with knapsack on back, stick in hand, and gun on shoulder, than an Indian prince travelling with all the ceremonial which his rank requires.

"You can't call it a man going from one town to another," said Banks to me; "it's a whole village altering its geographical relations!"

"I like Steam House far better," I answered, "and I would not change with this rajah's son for anything!"

"Who knows," said Captain Hood, "whether this prince may not prefer our rolling house to all his large and cumbersome equipage!"

"There will be only one answer to make to that," cried Banks, "though I shall have no objection to build him a steam palace, provided he gives a good price! But whilst awaiting his summons, let us look round the camp, it is worth the trouble."

The prince's suite consisted of not less than 500 persons. Under the great trees stood 200 chariots, symmetrically arranged, like the tents of a vast camp. Some had zebras to draw them, others buffaloes, and besides these, there were three magnificent elephants, bearing on their backs richly ornamented palanquins, and twenty camels, from the country to the west of the Indus. Nothing was wanting in the caravan, neither musicians to charm the ears of his Highness, nor dancing-girls to delight his eyes, nor jugglers to amuse his idle hours. Three hundred bearers and 200 guards completed the company, the payment of whose wages would soon have exhausted any other purse than that of an independent Indian rajah.

The musicians, who played tambourines, cymbals, and tomtoms, belonged to the school which thinks more of noise than harmony; but there were besides scrapers on guitars and four-stringed violins, though their instruments had never been in a tuner's hands.

Among the jugglers were "sapwallahs," or serpent-charmers, who by their incantations chase and catch reptiles; "mutuis," very skilful in sword-exercises; acrobats who dance on the slack rope with a pyramid of earthern pots on their heads, and buffaloes' horns on their feet; and lastly, conjurors who have the power of changing old snake-skins into venomous cobras, or vice-versa, as the spectators wish. The dancing, or nautch-girls, are usually very pretty, and play the part of both singers and dancers.

Very decently dressed, some in muslin embroidered with gold, others in plaited petticoats and scarves, which they wave about as they dance: these girls are decked with rich jewels, precious bracelets on their arms, gold rings on their fingers and toes, and silver bells on their ankles. Thus arrayed, they perform the celebrated egg-dance, with really extraordinary grace and skill, and I hoped that I should have an opportunity given me to admire them, by a special invitation from the rajah.

Besides these people, there was a considerable following of men, women, and children, in the caravan. The men were dressed either in a long strip of cotton, called the "dhoti," or in an "angarkah," or shirt, and "jamah," a long white dress, which altogether makes a very picturesque costume.

The women wore the "choli," a kind of short-sleeved jacket, and the "sari," equivalent to the men's dhoti, gracefully folded about the body, with the end thrown coquettishly over the head.

Whilst waiting for their evening meal, the Hindoos lay beneath the trees, smoking cigarettes wrapped in a green leaf, or pipes filled with "gurago," a composition of tobacco treacle, and opium. Others chewed a mixture of betel leaves, areca nuts, and extinct lime, which possesses certain digestive qualities, very useful in the burning climate of India. All these people lived on good terms with each other, and only showed animation at the hour for a feast. They were like the figurantes in a theatrical procession, who fall back into complete apathy, as soon as they are no longer on the scene.

However, directly we appeared, the Hindoos started up and salaamed to us, bending down to the earth. A number also shouted, "Sahib! sahib!" and we answered with friendly gestures.

It occurred to me that perhaps Prince Gourou Singh might give in our honour one of those fetes of which rajahs are so lavish. The wide court of the bungalow was there all ready for any ceremony of this kind, and seemed to me admirably suited for the dances of the nautch-girls, the incantations of the charmers, or the tricks of the acrobats.

It would have delighted me, I acknowledge, to be present

at such a spectacle in the middle of a serai, beneath the shade of magnificent trees, and with the natural get-up of the attendants. It would all have been worth far more than the boards of a narrow theatre, with its scenery of painted canvas, and its imitation trees.

I spoke my thoughts to my companions, who, while sharing my desire, did not think it would be realized.

"The Rajah of Guzarate," said Banks, is an independent man, who was with difficulty induced to submit, after the sepoy revolt, during which his conduct was at least suspicious. He does not at all like the English, and his son is not likely to make himself agreeable."

"Well, well, we can do without his nautchs," responded Captain Hood, shrugging his shoulders disdainfully.

Bank's idea was probably correct, for we were not even admitted to the interior of the serai. Perhaps Prince Gourou Singh expected an official visit from the colonel; but as Sir Edward Munro had nothing to ask from this personage, he expected nothing, and did not trouble himself.

We now all returned to our own camp, where we did justice to the excellent dinner Monsieur Parazard served up. Preserved meats now formed the staple of our food. For several days the bad weather had prevented our hunting; but our cook was a clever man, and under his knowing hands, preserved vegetables and meat resumed all their natural flavour and freshness.

ONE AGAINST THREE.

In spite of what Banks had said, a feeling of curiosity led me to wait all that evening for an invitation which never came. Captain Hood joked about my taste for ballets in the open-air, and even assured me that it was "no end better" than the opera; but of this, unless the prince showed himself a little amiable, I should have no opportunity of judging.

It was settled that our departure should take place at break of day the next morning, the 18th of June.

At five o'clock, Kâlouth began to make up the fires. Our elephant, which had been detached from the rest of the train, stood about fifty paces off, and the engine-driver was busy taking in water.

Whilst this was going on, we strolled about beside the stream.

Forty minutes later the boiler was sufficiently under pressure, and Storr had begun to back, when a party of Hindoos approached.

These were five or six richly dressed men, in white robes, silk tunics, and gold embroidered turbans. A dozen guards armed with muskets and sabres accompanied them, one of the soldiers bearing a crown of green leaves, which showed the presence of some important person.

This important person was no other than Prince Gourou Singh himself, a man of some thirty-five years, with a very haughty expression, of a type common among the rajahs, in whose features are often found traces of the Mahratta character.

The prince did not deign to take notice of our presence. He walked forward a few paces and approached the gigantic elephant, which Storr's hand was now causing to move. Then after gazing at it, not without some feeling of curiosity, though that he did not wish to betray,—

"Who made that machine?" he demanded of Storr.

The engine-driver pointed to the engineer, who had joined us, and was standing a short distance off.

Prince Gourou Singh expressed himself very easily in English, and turning towards Banks,—

"Did you make . . . . ?" he forced himself to say.

"I did," replied Banks.

"Did not some one tell me that it was a fancy of the late Rajah of Bhootan?"

Banks signed an affirmative.

"What is the good," returned his highness, rudely shrugging his shoulders, "what is the good of being dragged about by a machine, when one has elephants of flesh and blood at one's command?"

"Probably," said Banks, "because this elephant is more powerful than all those of which the late rajah made use."

"Oh!" said Gourou Singh contemptuously, "more powerful! . . ."

"Infinitely more so!" returned Banks.

"Not one of yours," put in Captain Hood, who much disliked these manners, "not one of yours would be capable of making that elephant stir an inch, if he did not wish it."

"You say? . . . ." said the Prince.

"My friend asserts," replied the engineer.

"And I also assert it, that this artificial animal could resist ten pair of horses, and that your three elephants harnessed together, could not make him move a foot!"

"I don't believe a word of it," replied the prince.

"Then you are quite wrong not to believe a word of it," replied Captain Hood.

"And if your highness chooses to name a price," added Banks, "I will engage to supply you with one that will have the strength of twenty of the best elephants in your stables!"

"It is easy to say so," replied Gourou Singh dryly.

"And it is easy to do so," returned Banks.

The prince began to get exasperated. It was plain to see, that he could not stand contradiction.

"Can the experiment be made here," he asked, after a moment's thought.

"It can," replied the engineer.

"I should like," added Prince Gourou Singh, "to make this experiment the subject of a considerable wager, unless you draw back at the fear of losing it, as no doubt your elephant will draw back, when he has to struggle with mine."

"Behemoth draw back?" exclaimed Captain Hood. "Who dares to say Behemoth will draw back?"

"I do," returned Gourou Singh.

"And what sum will your highness wager?" asked the engineer, folding his arms.

"Four thousand rupees," replied the prince, "if you have got four thousand rupees to lose."

This would amount to nearly 400*l*. The stake was considerable, and I could see that Banks, confident as he was, did not much care to risk such a sum:

As for Captain Hood, he would have betted double that, if his modest pay would have allowed such a proceeding.

"You refuse?" at last said his highness, to whom 4000 rupees merely represented the price of a passing fancy, "you are afraid to risk it?"

"Done," exclaimed Colonel Munro, who had just approached, and now uttered this single word which was of much consequence to us.

"Will Colonel Munro wager 4000 rupees?" inquired Prince Gourou Singh.

"Or even ten thousand," answered Sir Edward, "if that would suit your highness better."

"Be it so!" replied Gourou Singh.

This was becoming interesting. The engineer grasped the colonel's hand, as if to thank him for saving him from the affront offered by the haughty rajah; but his brows knit for a moment, and I wondered whether he might not have presumed too much on the mechanical power of his apparatus.

Captain Hood had no such fears, he beamed all over, rubbed his hands, and advancing towards the elephant,—

"Attention, Behemoth," he cried, "you have to work for the honour of old England, remember."

All our party stood together, at the side of the road. About a hundred Hindoos left their own camp, and ran to be present at the forthcoming trial.

Banks left us and mounted into the howdah beside Storr, who by means of an artificial draught, was blowing up the furnaces so as to send a jet of vapour through Behemoth's trunk.

Whilst this was going on, at a sign from the prince, several of his servants went to the serai, and brought back the three elephants, freed from all their travelling harness. They were magnificent beasts, natives of Bengal, and much taller than their brethren of Southern India. The sight of these superb animals, in all their pride of strength, caused me a qualm of uneasiness.

The mahouts, perched on their great necks, guided them by hand and voice.

As these elephants passed before his highness, the biggest of the three—a regular giant—stopped, bent his knees, raised his trunk, and saluted the prince like the well-trained courtier that he was. He with his two companions then approached Behemoth, whom they apparently regarded with astonishment, mingled with some fear.

Strong iron chains were fixed to the tender of our elephant.

I confess my heart beat quick. Captain Hood gnawed his moustache and fidgetted about with anxiety.

Colonel Munro was calm enough, far calmer indeed than Prince Gourou Singh.

"We are ready," said the engineer. "When your highness pleases—"

"It pleases me now," returned the prince.

Gourou Singh made a sign, the mahouts uttered a peculiar whistle, and the three elephants, planting their huge feet firmly on the ground, drew all together. The machine began to move.

A cry escaped me. Hood stamped.

"Put on the brakes!" said the engineer quietly, turning to the driver.

And with a quick turn, followed by a rush of steam, the atmospheric brake was instantly brought to bear.

Behemoth stopped, immovable.

The mahouts excited the three elephants, who with straining muscles, renewed their efforts. All was in vain. Our elephant appeared rooted to the ground.

Prince Gourou Singh bit his lip till the blood came.

Captain Hood clapped his hands.

"Forward!" cried Banks.

"Yes, forward," repeated the captain, "forward!"

The regulator was opened wide, great puffs of vapour issued from the trunk, the wheels turned slowly round, and the three elephants, notwithstanding their struggles, were drawn backwards, making deep ruts in the ground as they went.

"Go ahead! go ahead!" yelled Captain Hood.

And as Behemoth still moved forward, the enormous animals fell over on their sides, and were thus dragged some twenty feet, without apparently making any difference to our elephant.

"Hurrah! hurrah! hurrah!" shouted the captain, who could not contain himself. "They might fasten the whole serai on to his highness's elephants! It wouldn't weigh more than a cherry to our Behemoth!"

Colonel Munro made a sign. Banks closed the regulator, and the machine stopped.

Anything more piteous to behold than the prince's three elephants now, could not be seen. There they lay, their trunks covered with mud, their great feet waving helplessly in the air, like gigantic beetles turned on their backs!

The prince, both irritated and ashamed, had by this

time departed, without waiting for the end of the experiment

The three elephants were now unharnessed.

They rose, visibly humiliated by their defeat. As they repassed Behemoth, the largest, in spite of his driver, could not help bowing his knees and saluting with his trunk, just as he had done to Prince Gourou Singh.

In a quarter of an hour, a Hindoo, the "kâmdar," or secretary of his highness, appeared in our camp and handed to the Colonel a bag containing the lost wager of ten thousand rupees.

Sir Edward took the bag, but tossed it scornfully back, saying,—

"For the people of his highness!"

Then turning on his heel, he walked quietly into Steam House.

No better way could have been devised for putting down this arrogant prince who had so contemptuously provoked us.

Behemoth being now in his place, Banks gave the signal and we started off at full speed, in the midst of an enormous crowd of amazed and wondering Hindoos.

Shouts and cries saluted us, and soon a turn of the road hid Prince Gourou Singh's camp and serai from our sight.

The next day, Steam House began to ascend an acclivity which connects the level country with the base of the Himalayan frontier.

This was mere child's play to our Behemoth, whose twenty-four horse power had enabled him successfully to cope with Prince Gourou Singh's three elephants. He pressed easily up the steep roads of this region, without its being found necessary to increase the regular pressure of steam.

It was indeed a strange sight, to see our colossal animal breasting the hill, giving vent to snorts and shrieks as he dragged our train up after him. Our heavy wheels crashed and ground along, not, it must be confessed, to the improvement of the roads; in which already softened by torrents of rain, they made deep ruts. In spite of it all, Steam House gradually rose, the panorama widened, the plain subsided, and towards the south the horizon stretched at last further than the eye could reach.

We were more sensible of the effect produced when for some hours, the road lay under the trees of a thick forest. Now and then a wide glade opened before us, like an immense window on the mountain ridge, when we would stop our train, for a minute or two if the landscape was misty, or for half a day, if the view was clear. All four then leaning out of the back verandah would take our fill of gazing at the magnificent panorama extended before our eyes.

This ascent, interrupted by more or less prolonged halts —for the view as well as for night encampments—continued for no less than seven days, from the 19th to the 25th of June.

"With a little patience," remarked Captain Hood, "our train will mount to the very highest summits of the Himalayas!"

"Don't be too ambitious, captain," responded the engineer.

"It could do it, Banks!"

"Yes, Hood, it could if the practicable road did not soon come to an end, and provided we carried fuel, for that we should no longer find amongst the glaciers, besides respirable air, which would be wanting up there. But there is no need for us to do more than just pass the habitable zone of the Himalayas. When Behemoth has attained a medium altitude, he will stop in some pleasant spot, on the border of an Alpine-like forest, in delicious air refreshed by the breezes from above. Our friend Munro will have transported his Calcutta bungalow on to the mountains of Nepaul, that is all, and there we can stay as long as we like."

On the 25th of June, we found the halting-place in which we were to camp for several months. For forty-eight hours the road had been becoming less and less practicable, being either half-made or deeply cut up by the rain. It was a regular tug for Behemoth, but he managed it by devouring a little more fuel than usual. A few pieces of wood, added to Kâlouth's furnace, served to increase the steam pressure.

For this last forty-eight hours our train had been travelling through an almost deserted country. Settlements or villages were no longer to be met with. Only here and there a farm, or isolated dwelling, buried in the great pine-forests, with which the southern ridges bristled. Three or four times a solitary mountaineer greeted us with admiring exclamations. No doubt, on seeing the marvellous apparatus ascending the mountain, they imagined that Brahma had taken it into his head to transport an entire pagoda to some inaccessible and lofty height.

At last, on the 25th of June, Banks gave the word to "Halt!" and thus ended the first part of our journey into Northern India.

The train came to a standstill in the middle of a wide glade, near a torrent, the limpid waters of which would supply the wants of our camp for several months. Our out-look, too, extended for fifty or sixty miles over the plain.

Steam House was now 975 miles from its starting-place, 6000 feet above the level of the sea, and resting at the foot of the Dhawalagiri, whose summit rises 27,000 feet into the air.

CHAPTER XV.

THE PÂL OF TANDÎT.

HAVING followed thus far the travels of Colonel Munro and his companions, from Calcutta to the Indo-Chinese frontier, and seen them safely encamped at the base of the mountains of Thibet, we will leave them for a time in their winter-quarters and devote a few pages to some other characters who have appeared in our story.

Our readers may remember the incident which marked the arrival of Steam House at Allahabad. From a newspaper of that town, dated the 25th of May, Colonel Munro learnt the news of the death of Nana Sahib. Was this report so often spread before, and again so often contradicted, this time indeed true? After reading such minute details, could Sir Edward Munro still doubt, and was he not justified in renouncing all expectation of being able finally to do justice on the rebel of 1857?

We shall be enabled to judge of this, when we hear of all that occurred after the night of the 7th of March, during which Nana Sahib, accompanied by Balao Rao, his brother, and escorted by most faithful companions, the Hindoo Kalagani amongst the number, left the caves of Adjuntah.

Sixty hours later, the Nabob reached the narrow defiles of the Sautpoora mountains, after crossing the Taptee, which flows into the sea on the west coast, near Surat. He was then a hundred miles from Adjuntah, in a part of the province little frequented, and thus tolerably secure for a time. The place was well chosen.

The river Nerbudda flows between two ranges of mountains, the Sautpooras on the south and the Vindhyas on the north. These two chains are entangled with each other in such a way as to form most intricate and safe retreats. On looking at the map it will be seen that the Vindhyas form one of the great sides of the central triangle of the peninsular, about the twenty-third degree of latitude, but that the Sautpooras do not go beyond the seventy-fifth degree of longitude, and end with Mount Kaligong.

Here Nana Sahib was near the country of the Ghoonds, an aboriginal tribe, only half subdued, whom he hoped to induce to revolt.

Ghoondwana is a territory of two hundred square miles, containing a population of more than three millions. M. Rousselet considers the inhabitants to be always ripe for rebellion. It is quite an important part of Hindoostan, and truth to say, is only nominally under English rule. The railway from Bombay to Allahabad traverses this district from south-west to north-east, and even has a branch into the centre of the province of Nagpore; but the tribes remain as savage as ever, become refractory at any proposal of civilization, are very impatient of the European yoke, and in fact, as they can any moment retreat into their mountain fastnesses, are extremely difficult to keep in order, and this Nana Sahib well knew.

Here then he determined to seek shelter, so as to escape the search of the English police, and there to await a fit time to provoke an insurrectional movement.

If the Nabob should succeed in his enterprise, if at his summons the Ghoonds should rise and follow where he led, the revolt would doubtless spread rapidly and widely.

To the north of Ghoondwana lies Bundelcund, which comprises the mountainous region, situated between the higher plateau of the Vindhyas and the important river the Jumna. In this country, covered with beautiful virgin forests, live a deceitful and cruel people, among whom all criminals, political or otherwise, seek and easily find a refuge. These provinces still remain barbarous, and here still live the descendants of those who fought under Tippoo Sahib against the invaders. Here, too, are the head-quarters of the celebrated stranglers, the Thugs, so long the terror of India, fanatical assassins, who destroy innumerable victims, though without shedding blood; as well as bands of Pindarris, who perpetrate the most odious massacres, almost with impunity. In every part are swarms of the terrible Dacoits, a sect of poisoners, who follow in the footsteps of the Thugs; and finally Nana Sahib himself had taken refuge here, after escaping the royal troops, now masters of Jansi. He having thus thrown them off the scent, intended soon to go and seek a more secure asylum in the inaccessible retreats of the Indo-Chinese frontier.

To the east of Ghoondwana, is Kondistan or the country of the Konds. These people are the fierce votaries of Tado Pennor, the god of the earth, and Maunek Soro, the red god of battles. They are much given to those "meriahs" or human sacrifices, which the English have so long endeavoured to abolish; and can only be compared to the savage natives of the most barbarous Polynesian islands. In 1840 and 1854, Major-General John Campbell with Captains Macpherson, Macvicar, and Fry, engaged in long and troublesome expeditions against these daring fanatics, who will do anything under a religious pretext, if an unscrupulous leader can be found.

To the west of Ghoondwana, lies a state containing from 1,500,000 to 2,000,000 souls, occupied by the Bheels, formerly so powerful in Malwa and Rajpootana, now divided into clans, and spread all about the Vindhyas. They are almost always intoxicated with the spirit they obtain from the "mikowah" tree, but are brave, daring, hardy, and active, and constantly prepared to answer to the "kisri" their cry for war or pillage.

From this description it will be seen that Nana Sahib had chosen well. In this central region of the peninsula, he hoped this time, instead of a mere military insurrection, to provoke a national movement, in which Hindoos of every caste would take part.

But before taking any decided step, it was necessary to settle in the country so as to obtain as much influence, and act as effectively as was possible under the circumstances. This, of course, necessitated the discovery of a safe retreat, for a time at any rate, which he could be free to abandon, directly it was suspected.

This was Nana Sahib's first care. The Hindoos who had followed him from Adjuntah, could go and come a they liked throughout the presidency. Balao Rao, who was not included in the governor's notice, might also have enjoyed the same immunity, had it not been for his likeness to his brother. Since his flight to the frontiers of Nepaul, attention had not been drawn to his person, and there was every reason to believe him dead. But, taken for Nana Sahib, he would have been at once arrested, and this at any cost. must be avoided.

A single asylum then was needed for these two brothers, one in thought and aim, and in the defiles of the Sautpoora Mountains, this would neither take long nor be difficult to find.

A suitable place was at last pointed out by one of the natives of the band, a Ghoond, who knew every inch of the valley, even to its innermost retreats.

On the right bank of a little tributary of the Nerbudda was a deserted pâl, called the Pâl of Tandît.

A pâl is something less than a village and scarcely a hamlet, merely a collection of huts, or sometimes even a solitary habitation. The wanderers who inhabit it take up their abode there only for a time. After burning a few trees, the cinders of which improve the ground for a time, the Ghoond and his friends construct a dwelling. As the country is anything but safe, the house has all the appearance of a little fort. It is surrounded by palisades, and is capable of being defended against a surprise. Besides which, hidden in some thick clump of trees, or buried, so to speak, in a bower of cactus and brushwood, it is no easy matter to discover it at all.

Usually, the pâl crowns some hillock with a narrow valley on one side, between two steep spurs of the mountains, in the midst of an impenetrable forest. It does not seem that any human creature could live there. There is no road to it, nor even the vestige of a path. To reach one, it is sometimes necessary to ascend the bed of a torrent, so that the water may wash away all traces of any one having passed that way. In the warm season, men go up to their ankles in the water, in the cold season up to their knees. Besides this, a perfect avalanche of stones and rocks is kept ready at the top, arranged so that even a child's hand would be sufficient to push them over, and crush any one who attempted to reach the pâl against the wish of the inhabitants.

Isolated as they are in their inaccessible eyries, the Ghoonds can yet communicate most rapidly from pâl to pâl. From the unequal ridges of the Sautpooras, signals are in a few minutes sent over sixty miles of country. A fire lighted on the summit of a pointed rock, a tree changed into a gigantic torch, a column of smoke on the top of a spur of the hills: the inhabitants all know what these signify. The enemy, that is to say, a detachment of English soldiers, or a squad of police, has penetrated into the valley, ascended the course of the Nerbudda, is searching the gorges, in quest of some criminal, to whom the district offers a willing refuge. The war-cry, so familiar to the ear of the mountaineers, becomes a cry of alarm. A stranger might mistake it for the call of night-birds, or the hissing of serpents.

The Ghoond does not so mistake it, however: it is a warning that he must fly, and so he does. The suspected pâls are abandoned, or even burnt. The nomads escape to other retreats, to be in their turn deserted if close pressed, so that when the agents of the authorities at last make their way to them, they find nothing but ruins.

It was to one of these places, the Pâl of Tandît, that Nana Sahib and his friends came to take refuge. The faithful Ghoond, so devoted to the person of the nabob, brought them to it, and there, on the 12th of March, they stationed themselves.

The brothers' first care, after taking possession of the Pâl of Tandît, was diligently to reconnoitre the neighbourhood. They observed in what directions they could see, and how far. They found out what were the nearest habitations, and who were their occupants. The position of this lonely peak, on which in the midst of a group of trees, was the Pâl of Tandît, was minutely studied, until they finally came to the conclusion that it was utterly impossible to obtain access to it without following the bed of the Nazzur torrent, up which they had themselves ascended.

The security this Pâl offered was undoubted, more especially as below it was a cave or tunnel, from which secret passages led out from the spur of the mountain, and afforded another way of escape when necessary.

It was not enough, however, for Balao Rao to know only what the Pâl of Tandît was at the present time; he wished to know what it had been, and whilst the nabob was examining the interior he continued to interrogate the Ghoond.

"A few questions more," he said. "For how long has this pâl been deserted?"

"For more than a year," replied the Ghoond.

"Who last inhabited it?"

"A wandering family, who only stayed there a few months."

"Why did they leave it?"

"Because the soil did not supply them with sufficient nourishment on which to subsist."

"And since their departure, no one to your knowledge, has taken refuge there?"

"No one."

"A soldier or emissary of the police has never set foot in this pâl?"

"Never."

"It has been visited by no stranger?"

"By none," answered the Ghoond, "unless it was a woman."

"A woman?" exclaimed Balao Rao.

"Yes, a woman, who has been wandering about in the valley of the Nerbudda for the last three years."

"Who is she?"

"I have no idea who she is," replied the man. "Where she comes from I cannot tell, and not a person in the valley knows more than I do about the matter. Whether she is a foreigner, or a native, no one has ever been able to find out."

Balao Rao reflected for a moment, then resumed,—

"What does this woman do?" he asked

"She goes to and fro," replied the Ghoond, "and lives entirely on alms. Every one in the valley has a kind of superstitious veneration for her. I have several times myself received her in my own pâl. She never speaks, and is generally supposed to be dumb, and I should not be surprised if she were. At night she may be seen straying about, holding a lighted torch in her hand. For this reason she is always known by the name of the 'Roving Flame.'"

"But," said Balao Rao, "if this woman knows the Pâl of Tandît, is she not likely to return to it while we are here, and so cause us some danger?"

"Not at all," replied the Ghoond. "She is mad. Her senses have fled; her eyes gaze without seeing; her ears listen without hearing, her tongue cannot utter a word. It is as though she were blind, deaf, and dumb to all that goes on around her. She is quite mad, and madness is a living death!"

The Ghoond in the language of the hillmen, thus traced the portrait of a strange creature, well known in the valley under the name of the "Roving Flame" of the Nerbudda.

This was a woman whose pale, still beautiful, countenance, worn, though not with years, and quite devoid of expression, betrayed neither her origin nor age. The wild eyes looked as though they had closed to all intellectual life on some terrific scene, the horror of which still lingered in them.

The hillmen always received this poor inoffensive creature kindly. Like all savage people, the Ghoonds hold persons who have been deprived of reason in a sort of superstitious reverence. Roving Flame was hospitably welcomed wherever she appeared. No pâl was closed to her. They fed her when she was hungry, gave her a bed when she was weary, without expecting a word of thanks from the poor speechless mouth.

For how long had this woman led this existence? Where had she come from? When did she first appear in Ghoondwana? Why did she rove about with a torch in her hand? Was it to light her path or to scare away wild beasts? It was impossible to find out. Sometimes she disappeared for whole months together. What became of her then? Did she leave the defiles of the Sautpooras for the gorges of the Vindhyas? Did she wander beyond the Nerbudda into Malwa or Bundelcund? No one knew. More than once, when her absence was prolonged, it was thought that her melancholy life had ended. But no! She always came back, still looking the same: for neither fatigue, nor illness, nor privation had any visible effect on her apparently frail body.

Balao Rao heard the native with extreme attention. He considered whether there might not be some danger in the circumstance that Roving Flame knew the Pâl of Tandît, for, as she had already before sought refuge there, her instinct might lead her back to it. He therefore questioned the Ghoond as to whether he or his friends knew where the mad woman actually was at the present time.

"I cannot tell at all," answered the Ghoond. "For more than six months no one has seen her in the valley. Possibly she may be dead; but even should she reappear and come to this Pâl, there is nothing to fear from her. She is but a moving statue. She will not see you, nor hear you, nor know in the least who you are! She will just enter, sit by your hearth for a day or even two, then light her torch, and begin again to wander from house to house. That is the way her life is spent. But since her absence this time has been so prolonged, most likely she will not return again. The mind died long ago, and now the body must be dead also!"

Balao Rao did not attach sufficient importance to this incident to think it worth mentioning to Nana Sahib.

The fugitives spent a month in the Pâl of Tandit, and as yet Roving Flame had not returned to the Nerbudda valley.

CHAPTER XVI.

ROVING FLAME.

FOR a whole month, from the 12th of March to the 12th of April, Nana Sahib remained concealed in the pâl. He wished to give the English authorities time either to make some mistake by thinking he was dead, and so give up the search, or to go on a false scent in quite another direction.

The two brothers did not go out in the daytime themselves, but their faithful followers went forth throughout the valley visiting the villages and hamlets, announcing in ambiguous words, the approaching apparition of a great "moulti;" half god, half man, and thus preparing their minds for a national rising.

When night fell, Nana Sahib and Balao Rao ventured to quit their retreat. Following the banks of the Nerbudda, they went from village to village, from pâl to pâl, awaiting the time when, with some security, they might attempt the domains of the rajahs under British rule. Nana Sahib knew, besides, that there were many semi-independent tribes, who were impatient of the foreign yoke, and would rally round him at his summons. But in the first instance he must only deal with the savage populations of Ghoondwana.

These barbarous Bheels, nomad Konds, and Ghoonds, as little civilized as the natives of the Pacific isles, the Nana found all ready to rise and follow where he would. Although he prudently only made himself known to two or three powerful chiefs, that was sufficient to prove to him that his name alone would attract millions of natives from the central plateau of Hindoostan.

When the two brothers met again in their pâl, they compared notes of all that they had seen, heard, and done. Their companions then joined them, bringing from all parts word that the spirit of revolt was blowing like a tempest through the Nerbudda valley. The Ghoonds only longed to be allowed to yell the "kisri," or war-cry of the hillmen, and hurl themselves like a cataract on the military cantonments of the residency.

The time for that had not yet come.

It was in truth not enough that in the province lying between the Sautpooras and Vindhyas alone the spirit of revolt should be smouldering. That the fire might gradually gain on the country, it was necessary to carry the combustible elements into the neighbouring states, which were more directly under English authority.

The whole of the vast kingdom of Scindia, as well as the states of Bhopal, Malwa, and Bundelcund were to be made to resemble a huge bonfire, ready and prepared for lighting. But Nana Sahib, wisely enough, did not intend to delegate to others the task of visiting his partisans in the insurrection of 1857; those natives who remained faithful to his cause, and never had believed in his death, were constantly expecting his reappearance.

A month after his arrival in the Pâl of Tandît, the Nana began to consider he might act in safety. He thought that by this time the story of his having been seen in the province would be contradicted. Trusty spies kept him informed as to all that the governor of the Bombay Presidency had done to effect his capture. He knew that at first the authorities had instituted a most active search, but without result. The fisherman of Aurungabad, once the Nana's prisoner, had fallen by his dagger, and no one had suspected that the fugitive fakir was the Nabob Dandoo Pant, on whose head a price had been set. In a week the reports grew fewer, the aspirants to the prize of 2000*l.* lost hope, and the name of Nana Sahib began to be forgotten.

Without much fear of being recognized, the Nabob now began his insurrectionary campaign.

Now in the costume of a parsee, and now in that of a humble ryot, one day alone, and another accompanied by his brother, he went long distances from the Pâl of Tandît, northwards, to the other side of the Nerbudda, and even beyond the Vindhyas.

If a spy had followed him in his wanderings he would, soon after the 12th of April, have found him at Indore.

There, Nana Sahib, whilst preserving the strictest incognito, put himself in communication with the extensive rural population employed in the culture of poppy fields. These were Rihillas, Mekranis, Valayalis, eager, courageous, and fanatical, chiefly sepoy deserters, concealed by the dress of native peasants.

Nana Sahib, on the 19th of April, passing through a magnificent valley in which dates and mango-trees grew in profusion, arrived at Suari.

Here rise numerous curious constructions, of very great antiquity. They are called "topes," and resemble tumuli, crowned with hemispheric domes, the principal group being that of Saldhara, at the north of the valley. From these funeral monuments—these dwellings of the dead—the altars of which, dedicated to Buddhist rites, are shaded by stone parasols—issued, at the voice of Nana Sahib, hundreds of fugitives. Buried in these ruins to escape the retaliations of the English, one word was sufficient to make them understand what the Nabob expected of them; when the hour came, a signal would be enough to excite them to throw themselves *en masse* on the invaders.

On the 24th of April the Nana reached Bhilsa, the chief

town of an important district of Malwa, and in the ruins of that ancient place he collected men ripe for revolt, to whom he gave the news.

On the 27th he entered Rajghur, and on the 30th the old city of Saugor, not far from the spot where General Sir Hugh Rose fought a bloody battle with the insurgents, and with the hill of Maudanpoor, gained the key of the defiles of the Vindhyas.

There the Nabob was joined by his brother and Kâlagnani, and the two then made themselves known to the chiefs of the principal tribes of which they were sure. In these councils the preliminaries of a general insurrection were discussed and agreed upon. Whilst Nana Sahib and Balao Rao were pursuing their operations in these parts, their allies were no less busy on the northern side of the Vindhyas.

Before returning to the Nerbudda valley, the two brothers wished to visit Punnah. They ventured up the Keyne, under the shade of giant teaks and colossal bamboos. Here they enrolled many wild fellows from among the miserable people who work for the rajah in the valuable diamond-mines of the territory. This rajah, says M. Rousselet, "understanding the position which English protection gives to the princes of Bundelcund, prefers the rôle of a rich land-holder to that of an insignificant prince." A rich land-holder indeed! The region he possesses extends for twenty miles north of Punnah, and the working of his mines, the products of which are most esteemed in the markets of Benares and Allahabad, employs a large number of Hindoos. They are very hardly treated, condemned to the severest labour, and running a great chance of being decapitated as soon as their work is no longer required: so it is not to be wondered at that the Nana found many amongst them ready to fight for the independence of their country.

Leaving this place the brothers came southwards again, intending to return to the Pâl of Tandît. However, before provoking the southern rising which should coincide with that of the north, they determined to stop at Bhopal.

This is an important Mussulman town, and the capital of Islamism in India. Its begum remained faithful to the English during the time of the rebellion.

Nana Sahib and Balao Rao, accompanied by a dozen Ghoonds, arrived at Bhopal on the 24th of May, the last day of the Moharum festival, instituted to celebrate the revival of the Mussulman army. Both had assumed the dress of "joguis," religious mendicants armed with long daggers with rounded blades, which they dig into their bodies in a fanatical manner, though without doing any great harm.

Being unrecognizable in this disguise, the two brothers

followed the procession through the streets of the town, in the midst of numerous elephants, bearing on their backs "tadzias," or little temples, twenty feet high; they mingled with the Mussulmen, who were richly clothed in gold-embroidered tunics and muslin turbans; they joined with the musicians, soldiers, dancing-girls, young men disguised as women—a strange agglomeration which gave to the ceremony quite the look of a carnival. In this mob of natives were many of their friends, with whom the conspirators could easily manage to exchange a masonic sign, well known to the rebels of 1857.

When evening came, the crowd surged towards the lake which bathes the eastern suburb of the town.

There, in the midst of deafening cries, reports of fire-arms, popping of crackers, and by the light of innumerable torches, the fanatics seized the tadzias, and cast them into the waters of the lake. The Moharum festival was ended.

Just then Nana Sahib felt a touch on his shoulder. He turned and saw a Bengalee standing beside him.

The Nana recognized in this man one of his former followers. He gave him a questioning look.

The Bengalee thereupon murmured the following words, all of which were heard by the Nana without his betraying emotion by a single word or look.

"Colonel Munro has left Calcutta."

"Where is he?"

"He was at Benares yesterday."

"Where is he going?"

"To the Nepaulese frontier."

"With what object?"

"To stay there a few months."

"And then . . ?"

"Return to Bombay."

A whistle was heard. At the signal a native glided through the crowd and stood before them.

It was Kâlagnani.

"Go this instant," said the Nabob, "join Munro on his way to the north. Attach yourself to him. Render him some service, and risk your life if necessary. Never leave him until he is beyond the Vindhyas in the Nerbudda valley. Then—and then only—come and give me notice of his presence."

Kâlagnani signed an affirmative and disappeared. An order from the Nabob was enough. In ten minutes he had left Bhopal.

At that moment Balao Rao approached his brother.

"It is time to set out," he said.

"Yes," replied the Nana; "and before daybreak we must be at the Pâl of Tandît."

"Forward, then!"

Followed by their Ghoonds the two men skirted the

northern side of the lake until they reached an isolated farm, where horses awaited them and their escort. They were swift animals, fed upon spiced food, and capable of doing fifty miles in a single night. By eight o'clock they were galloping along the road from Bhopal to the Vindhyas.

The Nana prudently wished his return to the Pâl to pass unnoticed; so in order to reach their destination before daybreak, they pushed on at their utmost speed.

The brothers barely exchanged a word, but their minds were occupied with the same thoughts. During their excursion they had gathered more than hope—the absolute certainty that numberless followers would rally around them. The centre of India was entirely in their hands. The military cantonments scattered over this vast territory could not resist the first assault of the insurgents. Their annihilation would leave the way open for the revolt, which, spreading from coast to coast, would call up a wall of determined natives, against which the English army would dash themselves in vain.

The Nana's thoughts were divided between this and the fortunate chance, which would soon put Munro into his power. The colonel had at last quitted Calcutta, where he was so difficult to get at. Henceforth, none of his movements would be unknown to the Nabob. Without his suspecting it, the hand of Kâlagnani would guide him into the wild country of the Vindhyas, and once there, none could protect him from the punishment Nana Sahib's hate reserved for him.

Balao Rao knew nothing of what had passed between the Bengalee and his brother. It was not until they were approaching the Pâl, when stopping to breathe their horses for an instant, that Nana Sahib mentioned the subject.

"Munro has left Calcutta and is going to Bombay."

"The road to Bombay," exclaimed Balao Rao, "leads to the shores of the Indian Ocean."

"The road to Bombay, this time," returned the Nana, "will end in the Vindhyas."

This reply was significant.

The horses set off again at a gallop through the thick forest which covered the borders of the Nerbudda valley.

It was five in the morning, and day was dawning, as Nana Sahib, Balao Rao, and their companions drew rein at the foot of the Nazzur torrent.

The party here dismounted and left their horses in charge of a couple of Ghoonds, with orders to take them to the nearest village.

The rest then followed the brothers, who were already ascending the torrent.

All was still. The noise of day had not yet succeeded to the silence of night.

Suddenly a shot was heard, followed by many others; then shouts arose.

"Hurrah! hurrah! forward!"

An officer, with fifty British soldiers, appeared on the the crest of the Pâl.

"Fire! let none escape!" he exclaimed.

Another volley was fired straight at the group of Ghoonds which surrounded the Nana and his brother.

Five or six natives fell, the others throwing themselves into the stream, disappeared among the trees.

"Nana Sahib! Nana Sahib!" shouted the English, as they penetrated the narrow ravine.

All at once, one of those who had been mortally wounded, rose, his hand extended.

"Death to the invaders!" he cried, in a hoarse voice, then fell back dead.

The officer approached the body.

"Is this indeed Nana Sahib?" he asked.

"Yes, sir, it is," answered two of his men, who had been at Cawnpore, and were well acquainted with the person of the Nabob.

"After the others now," called out the officer.

And he with all his detachment hastened off into the forest in pursuit.

Scarcely had they disappeared, when a dark figure glided out of the dim recesses of the Pâl.

It was Roving Flame.

The evening before, the mad woman had been the unconscious guide of the officer and his men. She had entered the valley and was mechanically bending her steps towards the Pâl of Tandît, when she happened to pass a bivouac of these soldiers who were engaged in the search for the Nana. As the strange being glided by, the tongue which was supposed to be speechless, uttered a word, a name, that of the slaughterer of Cawnpore.

"Nana Sahib! Nana Sahib!" she repeated, as if some unaccountable presentiment had called up the image in her mind.

The officer heard and started. He instantly ordered up his men and followed in her steps, she appearing neither to see nor hear them. They reached the Pâl. Was this indeed the place in which the miscreant had hidden himself? The officer took the necessary measures for guarding the bed of the Nazzur and waited for day.

Directly Nana Sahib and his Ghoonds appeared on the scene, they were met with a volley, which laid many low, and among them, the chief of the Sepoy Mutiny.

Such was the account of the skirmish sent by telegraph to the Governor of the Bombay Presidency. The telegram soon spread all over the peninsula, the papers copied it, and thus Colonel Munro read it on the 26th of May in the "Allahabad Gazette."

No one could any longer have doubts about the death

of Nana Sahib. His identity had been proved, and as the paragraph stated—

"India has now nothing further to dread from the machinations of the cruel nabob who has cost her so much blood!"

The madwoman left the Pâl and descended the bed of the Nazzur. Her hollow eyes were burning with a strange light, which was not there a short time before, and she still muttered at intervals the name of the Nana.

She reached the spot where the dead bodies lay, and stopped before the one recognized by the soldiers. The horrid scowl with which he died was fixed on his features. Having lived but for vengeance, his hate still survived.

The madwoman knelt down, laid her clasped hands on the body, from which the blood flowed and stained the folds of her dress, and looked long and fixedly at the face. Then she arose and shaking her head, glided slowly away.

By the time she had gone a few yards, Roving Flame had relapsed into her wonted indifference, and her lips no longer uttered the cursed name of Nana Sahib.

8